*T*he phone rang, cracking the stillness, startling her.

She jumped, dropping the glass and spilling the remaining scotch on the hand-loomed pale carpet. She was across the room in seconds.

"Hello."

Silence greeted her.

"Hello?" She shrieked into the mouthpiece.

There was no sound on the line.

"Cyn."

She screamed. The receiver fell onto the inlaid, diamond-patterned cherrywood table, chipping a tiny piece from the edge.

Shaking, she turned.

He was standing there, a surreal figure in the darkness.

Cynthia Chapin-Rayner closed her eyes. . . .

By Judith Smith-Levin
Published by Fawcett Books:

GREEN MONEY
THE HOODOO MAN
RECKLESS EYEBALLIN'

Books published by The Ballantine Publishing Group are available at quantity discounts on bulk purchases for premium, educational, fund-raising, and special sales use. For details, please call 1-800-733-3000.

RECKLESS EYEBALLIN'

JUDITH SMITH-LEVIN

FAWCETT BOOKS • NEW YORK

A Fawcett Book
Published by The Ballantine Publishing Group

www.ballantinebooks.com

ISBN 0-345-42085-3

Manufactured in the United States of America

First Edition: December 2001

10   9   8   7   6   5   4   3   2   1

For KB
Who showed me the path, then
graciously provided company on the journey.

ACKNOWLEDGMENTS

My thanks and appreciation to:

Thomas Belezarian,
for his help in researching this novel.

and to:

Bill Kling
and
Loman Rutherford
Both of you were very good at making me laugh
until I ached. The memories are strong,
the smiles are many and the missing is constant.

God Bless.

TYGFMBTKNLAEIPA

PROLOGUE

She sat huddled in the chair opposite the fireplace. Across the room, the phone was silent on the table next to the two thousand dollar, high-tech massage chair she'd given her husband three Christmases ago.

She took a deep drink of the scotch, holding it in her mouth, letting it burn her tongue and throat as she slowly swallowed. She didn't like hard liquor, and knew she shouldn't be drinking it, but she needed something to stop the screaming in her mind. Her eyes watered. She wiped at them with the heel of her hand, like a child.

He hadn't called in over an hour.

She'd thought about unplugging the phone, or letting the machine pick it up but she couldn't. The calls had become some kind of mad contest. What would he say? Why did she want to listen? How could he justify what he'd done?

She took another deep drink of the whisky.

Her nose ran. She wiped it with the back of her hand. She couldn't believe what she'd become.

In the beginning, he had told her that he loved her joy, that she provided the sunshine in his life. Then he took it away. He drained it from her, until she no longer recognized herself. Who was this needy, whining soul wearing her skin?

She sipped the liquor again, and stared at the phone. Why didn't he call? She'd listen, she had to. There was something inside her that needed to hear every word. His words were as vital as blood, flowing into her veins. She closed her eyes and heard him, his soft, breathy voice. The sound, like music as it came from his mouth.

His mouth.

Sweet, warm, loving, wonderful . . . his mouth.

The memory of that mouth, those lips on hers, on her flesh, hit her so hard she trembled. A deep sob burst from her, shaking her body. The liquor in the heavy crystal glass spilled over the side and trickled down onto her trembling hand.

His mouth. It was his mouth that first attracted her. His lips were full, soft-looking and inviting.

She'd first seen him at a fundraiser for an inner-city women's shelter. She was sitting on a bright yellow silk damask sofa in Susan Sheppard's football field-sized living room, with the guest of honor, Gayle Bard. Gayle, a Seattle-based artist in New York for a show, had graciously donated one of her magnificent paintings for auction.

There had been an instant connection between the two women. Even their differences complimented one another. She in her tall blondeness, and the artist, red-haired and petite made a statement by merely sitting together. For Cynthia, it was like meeting a long lost sister.

Gayle had a "go for it" attitude. Even tragedy hadn't slowed her down. She'd lost an eye in a traffic accident, and now wore a patch, pirate-style. The pieces of fabric were different colors and designs, chosen to match her outfits or the occasion. Tonight's dark blue patch worn with a long, dramatic deep blue velvet dress, sparkled with real diamonds. A white gold, full moon pin at the shoulder completed the look. Gayle called it her "midnight sky" outfit.

While most of the other people in the room indiscretely disclosed their net worth in a never-ending game of one-upmanship, Cynthia and Gayle shared laughter and stories about their lives.

As they talked, the artist had taken her glass of Calfornia Chardonnay and ditched it into one of Susan's jungle of exotic orchids. She then produced a silver flask from her blue velvet handbag and filled the Waterford crystal wineglass with her own homemade concoction, Manhattans made with brandy.

"I would have brought cherries," she said, as she poured the liquor into the glass, "but they take up too much room!"

The two women laughed.

Cynthia knew the others would talk about her for "monopolizing" the guest of honor, but she didn't care. She hadn't been this close to someone who was this open and free in a long time, and *never* with this crowd.

In the middle of a hilarious story about the dedication of one of her pieces, Gayle stopped speaking, mid-sentence.

Cynthia turned to see what had captured her attention.

At first, through the crush of people, she could only hear his voice, a deep silky sound. She looked in that direction. It was as if she'd been struck by lightning. It was a good thing she was sitting or she would have fallen. Even so, her knees trembled.

"Oh my dear," Gayle said, sipping from the silver cup, atop her flask. "*He* is magnificient, the perfect subject." She smiled wickedly. "And afterward I'd paint him." She laughed merrily at her own words.

Across the room, he stood on the top step leading down into the vast, sunken room. His pale gray suit fit perfectly, draping just so over matching gray suede shoes. His face was turned away, as he spoke to someone standing close behind him.

Then he turned, his profile becoming visible.

Her breath caught in her throat.

He was dark, nearly blue in his blackness. He looked as if he'd been carved out of ebony.

She realized she'd stopped breathing.

As if in slow motion, the man turned more fully toward her. He was clean shaven, with high cheekbones and eyes that were nearly as dark as his skin. He had a face like one of those beautiful, carved masks of an African god, come to life right there in front of her.

His shoulders were broad, his legs were long, and she imagined the strength in the arms that muscled and rippled beneath the expensive fabric of his suit.

She was unable to take her eyes away from him.

He looked at her across the room, and she *felt* him.

Her body moved slightly on the silk damask, as if being drawn by a magnetic force. Her knees pushed forward, she leaned, every inch of her being moved, pulled in his direction.

It was then that *she* came in. Something inside Cynthia knew the woman was his wife. It was in the way she stood next to him, the familiarity with which she linked her arm through his.

Like her husband, the woman was also very dark-skinned, and as she looked around the room, her discomfort was visible. She didn't belong. Her dress was off the rack, and her shoes were cheap knock-offs of a pair of Manolo Blahniks that Cynthia herself owned in every available color.

As she stared, the woman looked at her, and their eyes locked. Cynthia closed her mouth and looked away, but only for a fraction of a second. Her head, without any word from her brain, instinctively turned again toward him.

The woman had left his side, disappearing back toward the entry hall, and he was speaking now to someone else. Again, above the other voices in the room, she heard his; her hearing tuned to its frequency, like a bat's radar in the darkest night. It was in that moment, *feeling* his words in a dark and neglected spot deep inside herself, that she moved.

She set her glass on the pale green marble-topped cocktail table and stood on trembling legs.

"Excuse me," she mumbled to Gayle.

The artist smiled and lifted her flask. "Good luck."

At that moment, he looked at her, and she began that long walk across the room. It was exactly like one of those old movies, where everyone and everything else disappears. She could see only him and his eyes on her.

"Hello," she said, her voice steady, her heart pounding.

"Hello." He smiled at her. The whiteness of his teeth against the darkness of his skin was devastating.

She extended her hand. The first touch of his flesh against hers sent a racing throughout her body that nearly collapsed her legs, dropping her at his feet.

"I'm Cynthia Chapin-Rayner," she said.

He looked both surprised and pleased. "Mrs. Dan Rayner?"

"One and the same." She smiled.

"Well." He continued holding her hand. "This *is* an honor."

"For me," she said, aware that his hand was still warmly wrapped around her own.

"I'm . . . ." Before he could finish his sentence, the woman was back. He turned to her, slipping his free arm around her waist and bringing her forward. "I'm Harlan Dubois Robinson, and this is my wife, Joyce."

The small dark woman nodded at her. She didn't smile, she didn't extend her hand. She just stood, her brown eyes fixed on Cynthia.

He smiled then. And she was again lost in the beauty of his mouth. His lips, his perfect white teeth. . . .

"It was that mouth," she muttered, her own lips touching the outside of the whisky glass. "It was that mouth that started the whole thing." She fell in love with his lips before she loved the rest of him. Kissing Harlan Robinson had done as much for her soul as a week in church.

The phone rang, cracking the stillness, startling her.

She jumped, dropping the glass and spilling the remaining scotch on the hand-loomed pale carpet. She was across the room in seconds.

"Hello."

Silence greeted her.

"Hello?" she shrieked into the mouthpiece.

There was no sound on the line.

"Cyn."

She screamed. The receiver fell onto the inlaid, diamond-patterned cherrywood table, chipping a tiny piece from the edge.

Shaking, she turned.

He was standing there, a surreal figure in the darkness.

Cynthia Chapin-Rayner closed her eyes.

Ernestine Henderson shot her husband Willis as he was enjoying his second cup of coffee for the morning. Well, enjoying maybe wasn't the word. He was complaining. Complaining *to* Ernestine *about* Ernestine.

She'd listened to this routine for twenty-two years. Usually the complaints were punctuated with a fist to the face, or a kick to the belly, or any other place he could reach.

This morning, he'd started in about the way she fried his eggs. The eyes were "too wide open." That led to how stupid and ignorant she was, and why did he waste his time with a "country sow" when he could "kick her ass back to Mississippi" and get a "real woman" to treat him the way a "real man" should be treated.

Ernestine had stood, listening and not listening to her husband. She was tired, having just come off the graveyard shift at the Hoffman Company, where she'd sewn hundreds and hundreds of zippers into blue denim pants for eight straight hours, starting at midnight and ending at eight A.M.

After work, as she'd done for the past fifteen years, she'd stopped at the supermarket and picked up fresh oranges and the morning paper for Willis.

She'd arrived home just as he was getting up.

While he showered and shaved, she removed one of his uniforms from the dry cleaner's bag hanging on the back of the bedroom door and laid the blue clothing out on the bed.

Next to the uniform, she set out fresh, clean white boxer shorts, spotless navy blue socks, and an immaculate white sleeveless T-shirt.

By the time Willis was dressed, she'd prepared his breakfast, squeezing the oranges by hand with an old-fashioned glass juicer. It had belonged to his mother and had been used to squeeze Willis's juice since he was a baby. It required that she impale a half of orange on its peaked center, and rotate it, until the orange surrendered its juice into the well at the base of the peak. Over the years, Ernestine had gotten very quick at extracting the juice, and she'd built the wrist muscles of her right hand into something that could open any jar, anytime, anywhere.

Willis didn't believe in electric juicers, he said they gave off chemicals that got into the juice. He didn't like fresh squeezed juice from the market either. He said the plants weren't clean, and God only knew what people were drinking. So, like his mother, Ernestine squeezed oranges every day, just enough to make one large glass. Thanks to her husband, she now hated orange juice.

By the time Willis sat down to breakfast, the complaining had already begun. She stood at the counter, listening to him whine about the "runny" eggs, while sopping the yolk into his toast, which had to be a "certain golden" color of brown, or it had to be thrown out (never eaten by her), and started all over again. This morning the toast was perfect, but the eggs were "too runny."

Ernestine leaned her hip against the cool white tile, her arms folded across her chest, her ankles aching, her back tired. She stood staring at the back of his head, listening to him berate her cooking, all the while shoving more and more of it into his face.

She knew what was coming next.

When he finished, he'd get out of the chair, grab her by the hair and slap her "a good one" just to teach her who was boss.

Ernestine's eyes shifted from the bald spot on the back of his head to the stove, and the heavy, black cast-iron skillet sitting there.

Willis didn't believe in Teflon, so she still cooked with the pots and pans his mother had used when he was growing up. For a moment, her hand actually twitched and her fingers flexed. She could feel the thick, heavy handle in her palm.

Her husband was nearing the end of his breakfast. He snapped his fingers at her. She dutifully poured him another cup of coffee, as he continued his rant, which in her ears had long ceased being words. Now, his grumbling sounded like a low buzzing noise—the hornets and yellow jackets she remembered from her Mississippi childhood summers.

Ernestine set the coffeepot back on the coffeemaker's hot plate. She stood there for a moment, looking at the dark, fragrant liquid. She loved the way this thing made coffee. Her mouth watered. She started to reach for a cup, but stopped herself. She'd wait until he left. That way, she could enjoy it in peace.

Even thinking back to how she'd had to beg him to buy the modern machine couldn't dampen her love of the coffee it brewed.

Whenever she drank coffee in his presence, Willis complained about the noise she made, even if she sipped and swallowed in total silence. He would glare at her across the table, and then go off on how this "piece of shit" coffeemaker made "lousy" coffee, and how nothing could make coffee like his mother's old percolator.

One day, praise Jesus, the damned percolator had just blown up and shot perked coffee all over the kitchen. Then and only then, did Willis allow her to buy this sleek, black (he insisted on the color) KitchenAid coffeemaker.

Ernestine stood, her hands flat on the counter, remembering the day they bought the machine, how embarrassed she was in the housewares department of the Village Discount Store.

Willis had opened every coffeemaker box on the shelves, and inspected the contents like he was mining for gold.

Her discomfort had continued when he finally chose one, and left the others open and disarrayed in the aisle. When she had suggested they put the machines back and close the boxes, he glared at her.

"That's what they got them assholes that work here for," he grunted, and set off for the checkout like he was on fire. She'd practically had to run to keep up with him.

At the register, he complained loud and long about the amount of money he had to pay for "such a piece of junk." Ernestine had been so embarrassed she wanted to turn into dust, like the "staked" vampires on her favorite TV show.

The young hispanic checkout girl, with the long red nails and the tattoo of a rose on the back of her key-punching hand, looked at her with such pity that Ernestine actually shrank.

All the way home, she'd had to listen to Willis's tirade. In all of his words, not once did he mention that it was *her* money, from *her* paycheck at the Hoffman Company that bought the coffeemaker.

Of course, the minute she brought her pay home, he made her count it out, and turn it all over to him. He let her keep twenty-five dollars "for emergencies," and if at the end of the week, she'd not used it for anything he considered an emergency, he made her hand that over to him as well.

Behind her, he belched loudly.

Ernestine's eye moved again to the big, black iron skillet, but instead of reaching for it, she turned and walked from the kitchen.

Willis whirled around in his chair. "Come back here," he yelled. "I'm talking to you, you good-for-nothing bitch!"

Ernestine continued down the narrow corridor, toward the bedroom, hearing his voice threatening its way down the hall. She went to the bedside table and opened it.

Willis's gun lay next to the roll of Tums antacid pills that he sometimes took at night.

Ernestine picked up the gun.

In all the years they'd been married, she'd never handled even one of his weapons.

It was heavy in her hand. She opened it, like they did in the movies.

The cylinder of the .357 Magnum was loaded with rounds. She closed it. The faint click of metal against metal sounded somehow comforting. With one last, lingering look at the smooth and lethal machine in her hand, Ernestine walked back to the kitchen, carrying it by her side.

Willis looked up to see his wife of twenty-two years standing in the kitchen doorway. Slowly she raised her arm, and pointed his .357 Magnum directly at him.

She held it like Clint Eastwood in those *Dirty Harry* movies, in one hand. Her *right* hand, with the barrel aimed at his head.

Ernestine smiled inside when she saw the shock on his face, and in his eyes.

Then he made a big mistake.

He laughed.

A bullet hit him right between the eyes, and a gamut of emotions crossed his face in seconds. Anger, shock, surprise, and finally fear . . . that was the one that stuck.

He toppled backward with the chair, landing on her waxed and gleaming cream-colored kitchen floor.

Ernestine stood there for a moment, amazed that she'd hit him. She'd expected the heavy weapon to kick. To waver and wobble in her grip.

It hadn't.

Her right wrist was *very* strong.

And Willis was very dead.

The hole in back of his head, leaking fluid, blood, and brain tissue attested to it. She wondered why they called it "gray matter" when so much of it was pink and red.

Ernestine laid the gun on the kitchen table and went to the counter. She poured herself a cup of coffee, and put cream and two sugar cubes in it. Then, taking a spoon from the silverware drawer, she turned and stepped over the mess on the floor.

Ignoring the river of red, inching its way across

the gleaming surface, she sat down at the table, facing Willis's overturned seat.

Ernestine inhaled the rich aroma of the coffee and stirred it gently. With a satisfied smile, she picked up the paper. She sipped her coffee while she read the front page, her horoscope, Ann Landers, and the comics.

When she was finished, she wiped her lips on a paper napkin, got up, cleared the dishes, and washed her hands. Humming, she stepped over Willis, picked up the kitchen wall phone and called Sergeant O.W. Greene, her husband's Commanding Officer at the Seventeenth Precinct.

Fat. That's what he'd called her. Fat!

Maxine Waterman laced up her two-hundred-dollar running shoes (truthfully, walking-at-a-fairly-good-clip shoes in her case) and cursed her husband Morton.

He'd flirted so much at their friend Letty's party last night, that she'd been humiliated. Whenever she looked across the room, there he'd be, his thinning hair combed over what he thought was a "small" bald spot, his forehead shining and him grinning at any woman under the age of twenty-five. They thought he was a clown, and she was just plain embarrassed.

After they'd come home, he'd gone on and on about the "beautiful bodies" of some of the young women at the party. He wondered if they worked out and how long it would take her to get into that kind of shape.

What did he think he had hanging over his belt? Gold coins? He was forty-six and he'd been chubby at eighteen. He hadn't improved, but she'd married him anyway. Now, twenty years later, he's telling her she's fat. That putz!

Maxine slathered a pumpernickel bagel with cream cheese, then added three thin slices of the lox she'd bought the day before at Stelmeyer's Deli. She took a big bite, wrapped it up in plastic wrap, and put it in the pocket of her red, fleece-lined jacket.

Noisily shutting the kitchen door, she stepped out onto the wraparound porch and took a deep breath of the chilly air. She actually enjoyed her morning "jogs" because they allowed her precious time to herself before she had to deal with Morty and the kids, although Roberta (who called herself Robbie) and Morty Junior, (who renamed himself MJ) barely spoke to either of their parents.

The crisp air felt good in her lungs, so she took another bite from the bagel sandwich, stuffed it back into her pocket and began her walk toward the woods near their house.

She walked for at least twenty minutes, thinking how much she hated everything about Morty. She even hated seeing him chew! Her anger was so great that she unthinkingly wandered deep into the woods, before she realized just how far she'd gone.

She was about to turn and head back to the house when she saw him.

A black man.

Running.

Her heart caught in her throat.

He was headed her way.

Oh, God! She'd left the stupid cell phone that Morty gave her on the kitchen table. What should she do? Where could she go? There was no place to hide. He was coming too fast. He was headed right for her.

As Maxine stood in the center of the small dirt road, the man came close enough for her to see his face.

"Oh, God." She sighed, and her body relaxed. It was Harlan Robinson. Criminal Courts Judge Harlan Dubois Robinson.

"Good morning, Judge Robinson," she called out, as he neared.

Harlan Robinson didn't speak, he kept running, his knees up, his head back, like the track star he'd been in high school and college. He passed her so quickly that the breeze blew her bangs back from her face.

Maxine turned, seeing the judge's back as he quickly disappeared into the woods.

"Gracious, you'd think the man could say hello."

She finished the last bite of her bagel and turned to start back. She looked at her watch. Morty would be just getting up, and she didn't want to even see him. She stopped, and turned in the direction from which the man had come.

"Well, since I'm in this deep, I might as well go see where this path leads," she said out loud. Crumpling the piece of plastic wrap and putting it back in her pocket, she walked deeper into the woods. Without the bagel sandwich for fuel though, and with most of her righteous anger at her husband dissipated, Maxine quickly grew tired.

"Enough of this," she said. "I'm going home."

She was about to turn when she saw something not far off in the distance. She debated whether to just leave it, but curiosity got the better of her.

In the blue-gray morning mist, curtained by the dying leaves of the trees surrounding it, the object looked like some kind of strange rock formation.

Maxine moved slowly toward it. As she got closer she could see it wasn't rocks, but something slumped and rounded in the misty air. Apprehension rose in her throat, but she kept walking. Her running shoes sank into the damp earth as she neared the thing.

When she broke through the last veil of trees, she saw it.

Clearly.

It was the last thing she saw until she opened her eyes and found herself cradled in the arms of a young, dark-eyed police officer, who kept telling her she was going to be all right.

* * *

Starletta Duvall turned over in bed, listening to the phone ring. She pulled the covers over her head, and tried to go back to sleep, but the sound penetrated her cocoon.

She sat up, yawning and rubbing her eyes. How long had it been ringing? Why wasn't the machine picking up? Then she remembered where she was. The sound of water running, from the bath just off the bedroom, brought her into wakefulness.

She reached out and picked up the receiver. "Hello," she said, her voice still clouded in sleep.

"Who is this?"

Star shook her head. "Beg pardon?"

"Who *is* this?" The woman's angry tone chased the last vestige of sleep from her brain.

Star leaned back against the pillows. "Who are you calling?"

The woman on the other end of the line slammed down the receiver.

"Ow!" Star rubbed her ringing ear and hung up. The phone instantly rang again.

She picked it up. "Good morning, Mitchell Grant's residence."

"Let me speak to Dr. Grant," the voice said. She recognized it as the same woman who'd just hung up on her.

"Dr. Grant is unable to come to the phone," Star said. "Is there a message?"

Silence greeted her.

"Ma'am," she said. "May I take a message?"

She could hear the woman breathing.

"Are you the *maid*?" she said finally.

"No," Star said, wrestling down the urge to say *"Are you?"*

"You *are* the person who answered a few moments ago, correct?" the woman asked.

"Yes I am," Star said, getting tired of the game. "Dr. Grant is in the shower. Would you like to leave a message?"

"Tell him to call his wife, *immediately*," the woman said coldly.

"I'll do that," Star replied. "I'll have him call his *ex*-wife, as soon as he's available." She held the phone away from her ear just in time to avoid another painful hang up.

The water in the bathroom stopped, and moments later, Mitchell Grant walked barefoot into the room. A lush deep blue Egyptian cotton towel was wrapped around his waist. His blond hair was wet from the shower, and drops of water glistened in the thick golden hair on his chest. He leaned over the bed.

"Good morning." He kissed Star softly. "Did I hear you talking to somebody?"

"Yes," she said. "Your ex-wife wants you to call her *immediately*."

Mitch ran a hand through his wet hair. "That can't be good." He looked at Star. "Was she rude to you?"

"She thought I was the maid," Star said, stretching.

Mitch smiled. "I'm sorry." He sat down and reached for the phone.

"It's okay." Star got out of the bed and walked naked toward the bathroom. Feeling his eyes on her she turned, and winked at him.

"Be sure and tell her I only work here because I really like the fringe benefits."

CHAPTER ONE

Sergeant Dominic Paresi poured his second cup of coffee for the morning and watched the double doors opening into the squad room. His partner was late. He stirred a spoonful of sugar into the coffee and added some cream. As he walked back to his desk, she appeared.

"It's about time," he said, sitting down at the desk facing hers.

"Good morning to you, too." Star took off her coat and hung it on the wooden rack behind her chair. "I had to go home and feed my cat. I'm ten minutes late."

"Ten minutes *really* late," her partner said cryptically.

"What's going on?" She sat down, facing him.

Paresi leaned forward, beckoning her to do the same. "Willis Henderson's wife shot him this morning."

"SWAT Willis- Henderson?" Star asked, her eyes wide.

"That be the man," Paresi said. "His wife put one right between his eyes this morning over breakfast."

"Yikes!" Star grimaced.

"Talk about starting your day with a bang," Paresi said.

She looked at her partner. "Point-blank, between the eyes? That's his speciality."

Paresi nodded. "Neat as anything he's ever done," he said. "I guess sharpshooting runs in the family."

"Between the eyes," Star muttered.

"Boom!" Paresi indicated the center of his forehead. "Third eye, for real. I hear it was so neat it could've blinked."

Star sighed. "I'm sorry to hear that." She looked at Paresi. "Though I was no fan of Willis Henderson's. Truthfully, I thought the guy was a jerk."

"You and everybody else with a brain," Paresi said.

"Yeah, but nobody deserves that. I wonder what made her do it?"

Paresi shrugged. "Who knows? The way I heard it, she plugged him and then sat down and had a cup of coffee."

Star's eyes widened. "Are you serious?"

Paresi nodded. "Sergeant Greene got the call. He said she was perfectly calm. She told him what happened, asked for a squad and a meat wagon." Paresi leaned forward. "Then she asked him how he was, and inquired after his wife and kids."

Star shook her head. "Sounds like she was either in shock, or totally unspooled."

"You be the judge," Paresi said. "She's here, in Interrogation Two."

"She's here?"

"Not only is she here," her partner said, "she's asking to talk to you."

"Me?" Star looked surprised. "Why?"

Paresi shrugged. "Dunno. All I can tell you is that Lewis has been running out here every five minutes looking for you, so I suggest you trot on in and see what's happening."

Star was on her feet. "Thanks for the heads up."

"Any time." Paresi watched her walk through the squad room and turn the corner, heading toward the interrogation rooms.

Captain Arthur Lewis looked up when Star entered. He glanced at the clock and back at her.

"Morning," she said. "Sorry I'm late."

"No problem," Lewis said. He indicated the small, thin, mocha-colored woman seated across the table.

"Star, this is Mrs. Willis Henderson."

Star sat down. "How are you, Mrs. Henderson?"

Ernestine smiled at her. The brightness of it unnerved Star, but she managed not to show it.

"I'm fine Lieutenant Duvall," the woman said serenely. "In fact, I'm better than I've been in a long time, and I'm really glad to see you."

Star looked at Lewis. She could see the woman's cheerful smile had the same effect on him.

"When Mrs. Henderson was brought in, Lieutenant, she asked to speak with you," Lewis said in the softest voice she'd ever heard him use.

Star looked at the woman across the table. "I heard what happened, Mrs. Henderson, and I'm very sorry."

"Call me Ernestine."

"Ernestine," Star said. "If there's anything I can do to help you, I'll certainly try."

Ernestine's eyes teared up for the first time. She reached across the table. Star took both her hands.

"My husband, Willis . . ."

"Yes?" Star said.

"He was a very bad man."

Star looked at Lewis. "Ernestine, I don't think you should say another word."

"She's right," Lewis said. "You're not under arrest, Mrs. Henderson, you haven't been charged. If you want to talk about the incident, you should have a lawyer present."

The woman's grasp on Star's hand grew tighter. "The officers that came to the house told me I wasn't under arrest, but they told me my rights, just the same. They said they just wanted to bring me in to talk."

Ernestine's voice grew softer, and her eyes darted from Star to Captain Lewis. "But I don't want to *talk* about it," she said. "There's nothing to say. I did it. I killed him, and I'm not going to lie and say I didn't."

"Mrs. Henderson . . . Ernestine . . ." Star said.

"No." A tear rolled down the woman's cheek. "No, Lieutenant, you got to hear me out." Her grip on Star's hand tightened. "My husband was a liar." She let go of one hand to wipe her face. "He was a lying dog."

Star looked at Lewis.

"Ernestine . . ." she said, "please, don't say anything else, let us get an attorney in."

"No." The woman wiped her face again, with her free hand. "I'm not going to say you didn't give me my rights. I was married to a policeman for twenty-two years, I know how it works." She looked at Lewis. "I know you all thought Willis was a good man, but he wasn't."

"Mrs. Henderson . . ." Captain Lewis said.

More tears rolled down her face. Lewis reached back to the table behind him and took a box of Kleenex. He slid it toward Ernestine Henderson. She ignored it, and continued to wipe her eyes with her free hand, while holding on to Star with the other.

"Willis was a liar," she said softly. "He was always a liar. I was the one who always told the truth, and I'm telling it now."

Her grip on Star's hand tightened. Star winced as the hold grew painful, but she didn't pull away.

"My husband did some evil things," Ernestine said, her voice so soft the two cops leaned in to hear. "I had to do it," she said, her eyes on Captain Lewis.

"I killed him." She looked at Star. "And *you* know why."

Star looked confused.

"Mrs. Henderson . . ."

The woman's eyes searched her face. "Ernestine, please call me Ernestine."

"Ernestine," Star continued, softly slipping her cramping fingers from the woman's grasp. "I don't have a clue as to why you'd kill your husband."

" 'Cause he beat me," Ernestine said. "I killed him 'cause he beat me." Her eyes again found Star's. "You know how he used to do me, you even came to the house, you talked to him, remember?"

Star tried to massage some feeling back into her hand. "I don't recall."

"It was a long time back," Ernestine said. "You were still in uniform. It was near Christmas, remember?"

Star looked at the woman and shook her head. "I'm sorry. . . ."

Ernestine leaned forward, her eyes boring into Star's, seemingly willing her to recall that long-ago evening.

"Willis had beat me real bad," she said. "You and your partner came in."

"Do you remember what my partner looked like?" Star asked.

"I surely do," Ernestine said. "He was real handsome, a fine-looking man. I remember he wasn't tall as you, but he was real good-looking. He had a mustache, and dark skin, but he wasn't a black man. He looked like one of those men from overseas, those men from the desert."

Star's mind raced back. "Tommy Bell," she said.

"Belezorian," Lewis said. "Tom Belezorian. . . ."

Star nodded. "Yes, I do remember now. I was riding with him then." She looked at Ernestine. "It was a couple of days before Christmas. There had been a big snowstorm, and Willis was really drunk. He had thrown the tree, the decorations, and most of the presents out into the snow."

"That's right." Ernestine almost smiled. "You and your partner came in, and he right away took Willis in another room, while you talked to me."

"That was a very long time ago," Star said.

"Yes, it was." Ernestine nodded. "I asked for you, 'cause you can back me up. You can tell them that Willis had been beatin' on me for a long time."

"If it continued after that night, you're right. That was more than twelve years ago."

Ernestine wiped her eyes. "I'm not saying that he beat me every day; he didn't. There were times when we had a good marriage, he'd be good to me, and then something would get into him, and he'd just beat on me for days on end."

She seemed to shrink inside her clothes.

"Last night, I got some really bad news at work, and I just wanted to go home, get him off to his job, and be alone. But when I fixed his breakfast, he started complaining." She pulled a tissue from the box. "I saw it coming. I knew he was going to start hitting me." She looked at Star. "I just couldn't take it this morning," she said. "I had to do something."

The hole was narrow, almost perfectly round, and deep. The woman inside was standing, her head slumped forward, her chin resting on her chest. She was naked. Her lowered head and pale shoulders were visible above the pit. Her body appeared blue in the morning mist. Bits of dried leaves, twigs, grass, and blood matted her long, curly, champagne blond hair.

Homicide Detective Charles Richardson stood looking down at the body.

Her blue eyes, open and unseeing, looked as if she were daydreaming—gazing at her white, pale feet, sunk into the cold dirt beneath them.

"Man," he said softly. "Just when I thought I'd seen everything." He crouched down, looking at the woman in the hole. Dark streaks of blood glowed on her bruised and naked breasts.

"Detective?"

Richardson looked up. A uniformed officer stood over him. "According to the description, we just might have an ID."

Richardson stood. "Who is she?"

The cop looked at the pad in his hand. "Looks like her name might be Rayner. Cynthia Chapin-Rayner. There's a house not too far past those trees." The officer pointed. "It's owned by a family named Rayner."

Richardson plunged his hands into his pockets. "That name's familiar."

"According to the info I got, she's married to some really high-powered guy, named Daniel . . . Dan . . ."

"Dan Rayner," Richardson muttered. "Hatchet Dan."

The cop smirked. "Hatchet Dan? What is that, some kinda nut-job killer?"

Chuck looked again at the body in the pit. He had gotten hooked on playing the market, even doing some day trading. He read every financial magazine out there. He was more than familiar with "Hatchet" Dan Rayner. The one-man tornado, who went around spinning factories and spitting out workers like a drunk losing teeth in a bar fight.

He faced the cop. "No, he's not a serial killer, at least not in the literal sense, but if you were a plant worker in any field, that name would have you shaking in your shoes."

"Oh wait." The officer snapped his fingers. "I think I heard of the guy. He goes around cutting the payroll, firing people at big companies."

"That's him," Richardson said. "He's a much hated dude. He makes his living off of shit-canning his fellow man. He calls it trimming the fat, when what he's really doing is putting people and their families in hell.

"Most of the people he gets rid of have years on their jobs. It's his way of keeping the companies from having to cough up all that retirement money, and the benefits that go with it."

"That sucks," the cop said.

"You got that right," Richardson agreed. "He doesn't give a fuck about who he's axing, he's just out to give those sleazebags who hire him a bigger bottom line."

He looked again at the corpse. "Of course *he* rakes in millions in salary and bonuses. He's got more money than God, which goes to show you that money can be a rotten thing." His brown eyes saddened. "But it won't help him here. Look at her . . . money ain't gonna fix this."

"Think maybe somebody made her take the heat for him?" the officer said.

"Sick as this is, you might be onto something." Chuck looked back over his shoulder. "How's the lady who found her?"

"Not good," the cop said. "She's pretty well spooked. It's not every day you find a dead woman stuck in a hole out here."

"Yeah," Richardson said. "Nothing *ever* happens out here. Money is a great cocoon." He looked again at Maxine. "Soon as she stops shaking, get a statement."

"Yessir." The officer hurried off.

The detective turned at the sound of a car pulling up. The black, city-issued Pontiac sedan came to a stop in the clearing and Dr. Mitchell Grant, the Chief Medical Examiner for Mercer County, got out.

After a wonderful night with Star, Dr. Grant found himself having a very bad morning. His ex-wife had informed him that his nineteen-year-old daughter, Robin, was "out of control" and that she was sending the girl to live with him for a while.

Ordinarily, he would have loved having his daughter stay with him. Indeed, he had fought for that right when he and Carole Ann divorced several years before, but Robin turned her back on him, and sided with her mother. Their relationship was strained. Now that Robin was practically an adult, Carole Ann wanted to hand her off.

He'd thought the day couldn't get worse, until he arrived at his office. He hadn't even taken off his coat when he heard the call. The body of a white female had been found in a pit in the north end of Hamilton's Woods.

Ordinarily, he wouldn't have taken the drive out to the area, but he knew Hamilton's Woods. The north end abutted the property owned by an old friend of his. So, with a cold kind of knowing, he drove to the site.

When he saw the group of cops and forensic people in the clearing, his heart began to pound. As he parked his car, and walked through the fallen leaves, it plummeted, making him light-headed. He could see the head and shoulders of the body, and even though the face wasn't yet visible, the wild tangle of curly blonde hair confirmed what he already knew instinctively.

Mitchell Grant had been a forensic pathologist for nearly twenty-five years, and the county's Chief Medical Examiner for the past fifteen. In that time he'd seen a lot of bodies and a lot of destruction. He liked to think he was immune to it, but deep inside himself, he knew better.

There were degrees of pain you could feel in his job. The deepest was for the children. The innocents who ended up on the cold steel tables of his autopsy rooms.

Though he was at a point in his career where he could be selective regarding his cases, Mitch often chose to work on the children. In his time, he had labored over children with all kinds of homicidal injuries. Bruised, battered, broken and abused bodies of all races and ages, from newborns to teens, had lain under the bright lights on his tables. He handled them all with a tenderness and caring that most had not experienced in their short lifetimes. Afterward, most of the time, he cried.

But there was something even worse than kids.

Friends.

Cops, city workers, colleagues. People with whom he'd shared laughs and a few beers. When familiar

faces turned up on his tables, the victims of someone else's madness, it destroyed him. Then Mitch
really went above and beyond his duty, working
until he was so tired, he couldn't see anymore. It was
these homicides that sent him to a bottle of Glenlivet
and time spent alone in a dark room.

"Morning Doc," Richardson said, stepping back,
allowing Mitch a space at the mouth of the pit.

"Good morning Chuck." He moved closer. A
muscle in his jaw twitched as he squatted down,
clasping his hands in front of him. He took a deep
breath. "Okay," he said to nobody. "Okay." Mitch
reached into his pocket, took out a pair of latex
gloves, and pulled them on. He raised the dead
woman's head. A look of profound sadness appeared on his face.

"You know her, Doc?" Richardson asked.

Mitch stood. "Yes." Two dead and dried leaves
attached themselves to the hem of his camel-colored
cashmere Versace overcoat. "She's the wife of an
old friend. It's Cyn . . . Cynthia Rayner. She's married to Dan Rayner."

"I'm sorry," Richardson said, truthfully.

"Me, too." Mitch looked around for the first
time since he'd arrived. His green eyes searched the
crowd of uniformed officers and detectives. "Is
Lieutenant Duvall here?"

"No sir," Richardson said. "She hadn't come in
when I got the call. Do you need to talk to her?" He
pulled out a cell phone. "I can get her for you."

"Please," Mitch said, looking back at the body in the pit. "I'd appreciate that."

"Done." Richardson moved a few feet away, dialing the number of the squad room.

"Homicide, Sergeant Paresi."

"Yo, Dom," Richardson said. "This is Chuck, where's your partner?"

"She's in on an interrogation. Willis Henderson's old lady plugged him this morning."

"No shit!" Chuck said. "Anybody know why?"

Paresi shrugged. "Not yet. She wanted to talk to Star, so that's where she is right now. If it's urgent, I can get her out."

"Tell her Mitch Grant needs to talk to her. We're at a scene in Hamilton's Woods. The vic is a friend of his. I guess he just wants to talk to her, you know."

"Yeah, right. Hold on Chuck."

Paresi put the phone on hold and walked into the interrogation room.

"Sorry to interrupt, Cap'n," he said. "Star, you got an urgent call."

"I'll be right back," Star said to Ernestine.

"Take your time," the woman said softly. "I hope nobody in your family is hurt or nothing."

Star patted her hand. "Thanks."

Out in the hall, Paresi filled her in.

"It's Mitch. He's at a scene with Richardson, and Chuck says he's pretty shook up."

"Thanks." Star punched the lighted button on her phone. "Hello."

"Hey Star," Richardson said. "Hang on." He handed the phone to Mitch.

"Star."

"What's wrong?"

"Can you get out to Hamilton's Woods, the north end, about half a mile in from Wells Road?"

"I'm in the middle of an interrogation, what's happening?"

"An old friend of mine . . ."

"Oh honey, I'm sorry," Star said.

"Thanks, but that's not why I want you here. You need to see this."

CHAPTER TWO

Star went back into the interrogation room.

"Captain, I've got to go."

Lewis nodded. "Don't worry about it. I'll take care of everything here."

She reached across the table and took Ernestine's hand. "Everything will be alright, Ernestine," Star said. "I'll look in on you when I get back."

"Okay, Lieutenant." Ernestine's voice was soft. "Thank you for being so kind."

"You're welcome," Star said. "I'll be back." She nodded at the Captain and headed for the door.

"Lieutenant?"

Ernestine's voice made her turn.

"I hope everything's going to be alright."

"Thanks," Star said. "I'll see you later."

Paresi maneuvered the unmarked car through the trees and down the narrow road to the site in Hamilton's Woods. They parked alongside Mitch's car. Star saw him, standing a little way off, his back to her. It wasn't until she moved closer, that she saw the pit and slumped head and shoulders of the woman inside.

"I'm here." She put her hand on Mitch's shoulder. He turned. The anguish in his eyes made her want to hold him.

"Thanks." His voice was soft and strained.

Mitch looked away. "It's Cynthia Rayner."

Star looked at the woman in the pit. "I'm sorry." She touched the sleeve of his coat.

He took her hand, briefly. His mouth turned down at the corners. For a moment, she thought he might cry.

Instead, Mitch cleared his throat. His sea green eyes glistened, but he blinked back the tears.

"You said she's an old friend?" Star asked softly.

Mitch nodded. "Yes, I was best man at her wedding. She's . . . was married to my old roommate at Harvard, Dan Rayner."

" 'Hatchet' Dan Rayner?" Star blurted out and was instantly sorry at the look in Mitch's eyes.

"I hate that name," he said.

"I apologize." She took his hand again. "I just never thought that you'd know somebody like that."

Mitch held her hand, not caring who might be watching.

"He wasn't always 'somebody like that,' " he said. "Danny was a great guy. We met at the Coop, in our sophomore year." He smiled. "We both reached for the last copy of *The Lampoon* at the same time."

"Who got it?"

Mitch's smile widened. "Neither of us. We started talking about how much funnier we were than the guys who put the thing together. We ended up going for a beer, and became roommates the next year." He shook his head at the memory. "Right from the start, it was as if we'd known one another forever. It was more like a reunion than a meeting."

"You must have had things in common."

"Lots," Mitch said. "We hung out at the same places, knew a lot of the same people, but we'd never met until that afternoon." His grip on her hand tightened. "He'd even lost a sibling, like I lost Livvy."

"In a car accident?" Star asked softly.

"No, not as traumatically, but just as painful. Dan's brother Jeff died of a rare bone cancer. He was just twenty-two. After that, Dan threw himself into a regimen of physical fitness that would have crippled a lesser man. Because of Jeff's illness and early death, he was determined to stay healthy and fit.

"He tried to recruit me," Mitch said, with a tiny smile. "I was athletic, but not driven. I played center on the basketball team, and Dan was captain of the rowing team. He tried to get me to go out for it as well, but those cold mornings on the Charles were not for me."

She leaned close to him. "Sounds like he was a wonderful guy. . . ."

"He was a *great* guy." Mitch looked at her. "But he had his faults. We didn't always agree on everything."

"Like?" Star asked softly.

"Money," Mitch said. "It was important to him, even then. He liked having it, he liked the status and power it gave him.

"We'd get into it sometimes because of his attitude. He could be high-handed with people who had less, and I didn't like that. In time, I grew to understand that his behavior came mainly from his insecurity. Coming from a wealthy family takes a certain knack for survival, and Danny didn't have it.

"His family could reduce him to nothing, so he put on that 'rich boy' face sometimes, but deep down inside, Danny was soft. The sight of a mother duck and her babies on the water could make him cry. But nobody saw that side of him, except Cynthia and I."

He looked again at the body in the pit. "You would have really liked her, Star. She was a radiant wonder. There was nobody funnier, or sweeter or better to be around than Cyn. Danny fell so fast, he left skid marks."

"Sounds like you liked her a lot yourself," Star said.

"I did." Mitch looked in her eyes. "Even though we haven't been close in a long while, she was always very special to me. I had a wicked crush on her for years. We used to laugh about it. But I never forgot that she was Dan's wife." He looked at Star again. "I just hope she didn't pay the price for it."

"Hey, babe."

The voice came from behind them.

Star turned.

"Tommy." She smiled, and moved toward the man. "Tommy Bell." They hugged.

"This is something," she said. "I was just talking about you this morning."

"All good, no doubt," he said, his dark eyes twinkling. He stood back and looked at her. "I haven't seen you in a long time. You look great, babe."

"Thanks."

He waved at Mitch. "Hiya, Doc."

"How are you, Tom?"

"Good . . . I'm good." He looked around at the site. "This is some ugly business, huh."

"That it is," Mitch agreed.

"So why are you here?" Star asked. "This isn't an arson."

"Not officially," Tom said. "But somebody tried to set the body on fire."

"What?"

"Hey, Star." Paresi's voice came from a wooded area, a few feet from them. "I need you."

"Excuse me," she said. "Hold that thought." She went toward the sound of her partner's voice.

"You said somebody tried to set her on fire?" Mitch asked.

"Yeah." Tommy nodded. "Let me show you."

Mitch followed him.

Star approached Paresi. "What's up?"

He pointed down at a line of white, shiny matter that appeared to trail from where they stood. It tracked through the woods and toward the pit.

"Whatdya think this is?"

She shrugged. "I have no idea." She looked back over her shoulder. "Maybe it's some kind of insect trail."

Paresi looked at her. "If there's a snail or a slug out here big enough to leave *this* trail, I don't wanna see it!"

"It's not insects." Tom Belezorian's voice came from behind them.

They turned.

"It's pool cleaner." He stepped carefully over the slightly iridescent line. "Watch your step, Doc," he said, as Mitch, directly behind him, stepped over it.

"Pool cleaner?" Star said.

"Yep." Belezorian squatted, and pointed. "It's a flammable chemical. I was just showing the doc. Farther back, it's ashy. That means it burned, and then fizzled out." He stood up. "As you can see, it goes all the way to the pit, and," he pointed, "there's some on the rim. That means whoever did this was going to try and burn her, but they didn't want to be close, so they set this up."

"Like a fuse on a stick of dynamite," Star muttered.

"Exactly." Belezorian moved in front of them. "See how it burned, stopped, burned and stopped?"

"That means whoever did this didn't stick around long enough to see what happened," Star said.

"Right," Tom agreed. "It also means the ground was wet when they tried to light it."

"It rained last night," Paresi said. "So she could have been dead when she was put in the pit, or she died sometime early this morning."

"She's in very early rigor," Mitch said. "I think she died just a few hours ago." He looked at his Rolex. "I'd say around five or six."

Still following the trail, Tommy led the small group out of the thicket. It ended, exactly at the mouth of the pit. The white chemical and its residue stopped at its edge.

"I'll bet when you pull her out, you're going to find more of the cleaner in the pit," Tom said.

Mitch looked up and beckoned one of his workers.

"Find out how close BCI is to wrapping up."

"Yes, doctor," the man said, and hurried toward a group of workers, measuring and collecting evidence.

"Nothing we can do, until we can move her," Mitch said, "and I want to get her out before the wet soil does more damage."

"Well, don't worry about the chemical evidence," Belezorian said. "Even if it leeches into the dirt, we can still get a sample." He turned to Star. "So, babe, you said you were talking about me this morning. What's up?"

Taking his arm, she walked him away from the scene, away from Mitch and Paresi. "Do you remember back when we were riding together?"

"With a permanent smile." He winked at her.

"Yeah, right," she said.

He laughed.

"Do you remember one night close to Christmas when we got a call at a cop's house? His name was Willis Henderson."

Tommy shook his head. "No bells, sweetheart."

"It was just a few days before Christmas. He'd beaten the hell out of his wife."

"We got a lot of those calls, babe."

"There had been a really bad snowstorm the day before, and it kept snowing off and on through the night. Remember, we had a car with a bad heater. We were freezing, and you kept suggesting we park somewhere and have skin-to-skin contact."

Belezorian laughed. "Hey, I read somewhere that's the best way to keep warm."

Smiling, Star raised an eyebrow. "Uh-uh. As I recall, that was your logic at the time. Anyway, the house was in that cute little neighborhood on Kingley Road, you know, those Victorians. This guy was a *cop*. In fact he was a SWAT guy."

Tommy rubbed his chin. "Oh yeah . . . now I remember, the sharpshooter. He'd kicked the shit out of her, tossed the tree, the decorations, *and* the presents out in the yard."

"That's the one."

Tommy laughed. "I remember you ducking when a life-sized, plaster Baby Jesus came flying through the door," he said, his memory flooding back. "If that thing had hit you, I would have had to shoot him."

"Well, talk about karma."

"What?"

"Do you remember his wife?"

Tommy nodded. "Now I do. She was a little bit of a thing, tiny, and he was this big bastard. I thought for a minute I'd have to stick him, till he calmed down."

"That's it," Star said.

"Yeah, so what's up?"

"She killed him."

"What?" Tom looked surprised.

"She shot him this morning."

"No shit!"

"Right between the eyes," Star said.

"Think he taught her to shoot?" Tom said, grinning. "I hear he could knock the dick off a gnat, during a hurricane, from fifty feet away."

"I don't know if he taught her, but she got off one shot, and it was perfect."

Tommy whistled.

"Now she wants me to testify that he'd been

beating her," Star said. "I guess she's going for the battered wife defense."

"Well he did her in pretty bad," Tom said. "At least from what I can remember."

"Yeah. But just think about how long ago that was. He must have been hammering her for years."

Tom nodded. "But it's over now."

"For real," Star said. "Anyway, I just wanted to let you know, you might be called, too."

"Thanks, babe."

Paresi approached them.

"They're taking the body out of the pit," he said.

Star turned. "We're there." They walked back to the site.

Cynthia Chapin-Rayner's dirty, naked, blue-tinged, and bruised corpse had been photographed and videotaped in its strange grave. Now it was laid out on a white plastic tarp. Dirt and mud smudged her belly, thighs, and legs. A twig had wedged itself between the bright red-painted, pedicured, middle toenails of her left foot. Two members of the Coroner's team began to fold the tarp over her body.

"Hold it," Mitch said. He squatted, removed the twig, and handed it to an assistant, who bagged it. He took her feet in his gloved hands, looking intently at the soles. He then gently rolled her onto her left side, exposing the back of her body.

"You're right, Tom," he said to Belezorian. "There are chemical burns to the bottoms of her feet and the backs of both legs." He stood. "The flesh is ulcerated, that means she was still living when she was put in the pit, and made to stand in the chemical, while more of it was poured on her."

Star saw the pain and the glistening of tears in his eyes.

"Whoever did this wanted to burn her alive."

CHAPTER THREE

When he got back from Hamilton's Woods, Mitch was in no mood to deal with anything but his own pain. He told his secretary to hold his calls, and locked the door to his office.

He sat on the sofa for an hour, barely breathing, his head pounding, while images of Cynthia and Dan Rayner raced through his brain.

Finally, he changed into scrubs and went down to the morgue. When he saw her under the lights, his heart hammered in his chest. He thanked the diener, waiting to assist, and asked him to leave.

Alone, he did the painstaking work of preparing Cynthia Chapin-Rayner for autopsy. The body had been weighed, fingerprinted, and tagged. Mitch photographed her, taking close-up shots of the chemical burns, bruises, cuts, and scrapes. He then carefully went over every inch of her with a high-powered light and magnifying glass, removing twigs, dirt, and any matter that could be tagged, bagged, analyzed, and categorized.

He cleaned beneath her nails, taking scrapings of the debris found there. He then clipped and bagged the nails for further examination. He removed her wedding ring and the diamond studs she wore in each ear, setting them aside to return to Dan.

As he worked, Mitch's mind drifted back to the past, and the fact that he'd once thought himself in love with this woman. He heard her laugh, and remembered how she never failed to make him smile.

Upstairs in his office Lorraine, his secretary, was calling every number she'd been given, trying to locate Dan Rayner.

Back at the squad, Paresi and Chuck Richardson worked the phones as well, while Star went to find out what was happening with Ernestine Henderson. Captain Lewis told her that Ernestine was being held in lockup. Knowing there was nothing she could do for the woman, Star went back to help Paresi and Richardson.

Harlan Robinson sat at the desk in his chambers. His hands shook, and sweat beaded on his forehead. He didn't feel well. He didn't feel anything at all. He looked at the calendar in front of him. The only thing scheduled for the afternoon was *voir dire* on the Hardaway case. It was open and shut, and if he tried, perhaps he could get out of the session.

He looked at the clock. He had almost an hour before it was scheduled. His heart raced. But then, if he left, it would draw attention to him, and that was just what he didn't need, not after this morning.

His stomach churned.

He was in no condition to take the bench. It wasn't possible that he could fall apart like this, not him, not Harlan Dubois Robinson. He had to get a hold of himself.

He'd been a judge for nearly a decade and he had a reputation. He was tough, and proud of it. He didn't have a soft spot anywhere for anyone who came before him. If they were guilty, they paid the price. He didn't care if they were rich or poor, black, brown, or white, he threw the book at them.

If a black man dared make eye contact with him, as if to say, "brother," Harlan handed down as stiff a sentence as possible. He didn't go for that "brother" crap. He'd been born blacker than a lot of those who stood before him, and it hadn't stopped him.

Harlan had dreams. From the time he could think and reason for himself, he wanted out. Out of the projects, out of the poverty. That thought became the driving force of his life. Yes, his pigmentation slowed him down, but he never let it paralyze him.

There had been no affirmative action for him, either. He came up the hard way.

His mother, Oletha, a nurse's aide, raised him and his sister Lynette, in a two bedroom apartment in the Jamison Projects over on Harrison Street.

Lynette got pregnant when she was fifteen. Despite a full schedule at school, Harlan pitched in to help his mother support his sister and his niece Arnelle.

He got his first job through a school work program, flipping burgers during the summer at a local fast-food restaurant. He worked at the burger joint from his sophomore through his senior year.

For a long time, the only money coming in was the combined minimum-wage pay from him and his mother. When Arnelle was two years old, his sister went back and finished high school. She eventually got a job working as a clerk in the Department of Motor Vehicles.

Harlan was determined to go to college. He saved as much money as he could, from his job at the burger joint, and spent every free moment he had poring over college catalogs. He researched grants and applied for every one for which he felt qualified. His track coach researched athletic scholarships, but Harlan didn't want that. He held that as a "last chance" if he couldn't get into college any other way.

He felt athletic scholarships were demeaning. They undermined your intelligence. To him they said, you got into this school because you can carry a football, or play basketball, or run, not because you can think. Near the end of his senior year, he got a grant from a private foundation. With that money, and his grade-point average, Harlan began his freshman year at the Amherst campus of the University of Massachusetts.

Even with most of his school expenses paid, he still worked throughout his college years. One of his jobs was as a busboy at the local country club. Talk about poetic justice, now he was a member in good standing of the same institution in which he'd once hustled, picking up dirty dishes.

He never forgot the way he'd been treated by some of the members who had been on top in those days. Now, some of the same palefaced bastards practically kissed his robes.

His hard work put him on the road out of the projects and into college and law school. It led him to a beautiful home in one of Brookport's most affluent areas, near Hamilton's Woods, and a seat on the bench of the Mercer County Superior Court. He'd become a powerful force in the city. In spite of his tough stance on crime and the criminals who came before him, he had a strong support system among Brookport's steadily growing middle-class black population.

In addition to being an extremely handsome man, Harlan had a mesmerizing voice. It could flow in soft, mellow tones, or it could thunder, like a mountain storm. He learned early on that he could persuade or unleash with that voice, and he was not above using it like an old-time Bible-thumping, Southern Baptist preacher.

His reputation was made shortly after he began practicing law. Though he wanted the gold, he set up his first office in a working-class black neighborhood. He soon developed the reputation as a pitbull attorney, who fought to the ground for his clients, and also won most of his cases.

It was during this time that, like most cities in America, Brookport was experiencing problems with a changing economy and a polarization of its black and white populations.

The assassination of one of the city's most vocal black voices, by a member of a white supremacist organization, had lit the fuse on a dangerous stick of dynamite, and it was Harlan Robinson who put it out.

He spoke to every group of blacks in the city. His voice rang from pulpits and street corners. He preached, charmed, and cajoled them to stay calm, hang together, and show strength. It was he who delivered the speeches that kept portions of the city from being burned to the ground.

After that time, Brookport's black citizens revered him, and the white ones realized he was not a man to toy with. It was the power of those days that started Harlan on his climb from his storefront office to the bench.

Brookport was an old city, with old money, and the memory of how he'd been treated by a lot of his current "friends and colleagues" had never left him.

Though he could be cordial, there were some that he hated, like Dan Rayner.

The Rayner family had been members of the Brookport Country Club since its doors first opened more than one hundred years ago.

Dan often came in with his family, and he always made it a point to lord it over the hired help. Even after he went off to Harvard, he still came to the club, usually bringing along some beautiful blonde from Wellesley or Smith College as his date.

Rayner liked classy-looking rich girls fawning over him, and he loved ordering people around, showing off his power.

The only time he was tolerable was when he came in with Mitch Grant.

Harlan liked Mitchell Grant, always had, even when he was busing tables at the club. Grant had always been a classy guy. In those days, Harlan studied him, his manners, the way he dressed, his easiness with himself and his wealth.

Years later, when they met on equal footing, Harlan noted that Mitchell Grant had an eye for the ladies. Though stories of his appetite were legendary on the city grapevine, Grant handled his affairs as he handled everything else—with class. Not so his friend, Dan Rayner.

Rayner's conquests were always boasted about. Some of the daughters (and wives) of the best families on the eastern seaboard were rated and laughed about at table seventeen, overlooking the golf course.

But Grant never boasted. He didn't have to. His reputation as a swordsman was fierce, and grew steadily, even during his long marriage. Recently, Harlan had heard through the courthouse rumor mill that the doctor, now divorced, had fallen in love with a black woman, Starletta Duvall, a Homicide Lieutenant who worked out of the Seventeenth Precinct.

Harlan knew Star, and he didn't like her. She had always annoyed him. There was something in her manner that set his teeth on edge. He had known and disliked her father, Sergeant Leonard Duvall, and to him, Star was definitely her daddy's daughter.

She had his long body, and freaky, gold-flecked, amber eyes. Those eyes had always creeped him out. It wasn't natural for black people to have eyes like that. They were spooky, like cat's eyes. Sometimes they even looked golden, and *all* the time, with Len Duvall, they mocked him.

He knew Duvall didn't think too much of him, either. He supported Harlan's views on education and self-sufficiency for blacks, but he thought Harlan needed more compassion and understanding, especially where poor people were concerned.

Harlan thought Len Duvall was a soft-hearted fool. He wasted too much of his off-duty time playing basketball and hanging with worthless kids on the concrete playgrounds in "the 'hood." It didn't do any good, other than to keep Duvall fit and trim, because most of the little bastards he was trying to save inevitably ended up either in prison or in the boneyard. To Harlan, trying to instill pride and respect in those people was like trying to empty the ocean with a teaspoon. In his opinion Len Duvall was a fool. A fool who died serving a department that couldn't have cared less about him. Now his daughter sat on the cop's bench in the courtroom and regarded him with her father's eyes. Still, he could understand why Grant would want her; she was beautiful. Even he had to agree to that. But she was still Len Duvall's daughter.

Harlan shook his head, wondering what Grant's old buddy, Dan Rayner thought about his blue-blooded friend falling for a sister. He knew that Rayner regarded blacks as pretty low on the evolutionary scale. He never came out and called anybody "nigger" but his attitude spoke volumes. Even now, when their paths crossed at some charity event, Rayner's manner could still make Harlan feel as if he had the words "property of" branded on his ass.

"But I showed him," the judge whispered. "I showed him."

He looked down at his shaking hands. "*She* loved me, no matter what. Cyn loved *me*."

Dan Rayner took another sip of his bourbon, and watched the eyes of the white-haired captain of industry sitting across the table from him.

"You mean you can save me *this* amount of money in a year's time?" the man said incredulously.

"You're carrying a lot of dead weight, Henry. I can trim the fat."

"And all you ask is?" Henry Knight said.

"My usual package, plus bonus." Dan pointed at the navy blue prospectus in the man's hands. "You can see what I do, you know my rep, and you know I don't lie. I can put your company back on track."

"But what about the employees who have been with me for most of their working lives?"

"What about them?" Dan asked coldly.

Henry looked uncomfortable.

Dan indicated the papers in the man's hands. "You're bleeding red ink, Henry. Why don't you let the doctor operate? What do you say?"

Before Henry Knight could speak, the ringing of Dan's cell phone cut short his words.

"Son of a bitch." Dan took the phone out of his breast pocket.

"*What!*"

He listened for a few moments, then his face went white.

He put the phone back in his pocket. Henry Knight noticed his hands were shaking.

"Dan, you alright?"

"I've got to go." Dan Rayner stood up, knocking over his drink, not noticing its amber color staining the white Irish Linen tablecloth.

"I've got to go," he said again, his eyes blank.

Henry Knight watched him weave through the tables, on his way to the door.

"I'll call you," Henry yelled out, but Dan Rayner had already left the restaurant.

CHAPTER FOUR

Dan Rayner didn't look like a "Hatchet Dan." In fact, he didn't look very much like anything at all. He was tall, slim, and elegantly dressed, with immaculately cut sandy, gray-streaked hair, which framed a face that seemed unfinished.

There was a blankness to his features that made Star think of the pod people in *The Invasion of the Body Snatchers*. He didn't seem to be fully formed. His countenance was so generic as to be forgettable. Looking at him, one could never imagine the carnage he'd inflicted on various companies throughout the world.

After spending most of the day searching for him, Dan Rayner had finally been found by one of his six secretaries.

He'd flown back to Brookport from New Jersey and had come straight to the police station. Now he sat in the same interrogation room that had been occupied that morning by Ernestine Henderson.

Star and Richardson sat opposite him at the scarred, green metal table.

"Would you like something to drink, Mr. Rayner?" Star asked.

"No." He stretched out his long, gangly legs beneath the table. His pale gray eyes went from her face to Richardson's.

Both black detectives recognized "the look."

Richardson's lips curved slightly.

"I just want to know what happened to my wife."

"We're not exactly sure, sir," Star said.

Chuck saw "Incompetent" flash in those cold gray eyes.

"What does that mean?" Dan Rayner said, his voice even and without feeling.

"It means, Mr. Rayner," Star said, "that the autopsy hasn't been completed as yet. We can only go by the appearance of your wife's body, and that isn't enough to give you an official cause of death."

"I want to see her."

"That's not possible," Star said softly.

Rayner stared at her. "I'm an extremely close friend of the Chief Medical Examiner, Lieutenant," he said. "I'm sure, if you call Dr. Mitchell Grant, he will allow me to see my wife."

"In due time, Mr. Rayner."

"Is there someone who can account for your whereabouts between the hours of ten last night and six this morning?" Richardson interjected.

"Am I a suspect?" Dan Rayner turned his colorless eyes on the detective.

Richardson returned the gaze. "We just need to know your whereabouts."

Dan leaned forward. "I was with Henry Knight at the Knight Tool Company in Newark, New Jersey."

Richardson wrote down the information. "We'll check it out."

Rayner's cold eyes never left the detective's face. "I flew in my *private* jet," he said, dismissively. "We took off from DeLiberti. The flight plans are on record. Once in Newark, I had a car and driver. I was never alone at any time. When we reached Henry's office, I was with him until I got the call saying my wife was dead. The pilot, the driver, and Henry Knight himself will all verify this information."

Richardson picked up his notebook. "Thanks." He turned to Star. "I'll check into this." He left the room.

"Thank you for being so forthcoming, Mr. Rayner," she said. "We're not considering you as a suspect, but we have to look at every angle."

"I understand, Lieutenant." Rayner folded his long hands. "My wife is dead. She was alive when I left home and now she isn't. Like you, I want to know why."

"Danny."

Star looked up at the sound of the voice.

"Mitch." Dan Rayner stood and embraced the medical examiner.

"I'm sorry," Mitch said, truthfully.

"Thanks." Dan Rayner embraced him again.

Mitch turned to Star. "I hope you don't mind my coming in, Lieutenant."

"No, not at all." She indicated a chair at the table, and Mitch sat down.

"I haven't done the autopsy as yet, Danny, but I've finished all the preliminary work. My secretary told me you'd been found, and that you were here. I wanted to see you," Mitch said to his old friend.

"Thanks." Dan Rayner's voice broke for the first time. "Thank you for coming and for looking after Cyn."

Mitch took his hand. "You knew I'd take care of her," he said softly. "I couldn't let somebody else do it."

"I'm glad." Rayner's voice was hoarse with emotion. "I'm glad she had you to be with her." He squeezed the doctor's hand. "Can I see her, Mitch?"

"Not yet, Danny," Mitch said softly.

A sob broke from Dan Rayner's throat.

Mitch turned to Star. "Would you mind if I had a couple of minutes with him?"

"No." She stood up. "Take your time."

When she left the room, Paresi was standing in the hallway, near the door.

"What's happening?"

"Mitchell wanted to talk to him alone," Star said. "Do you have any more information?"

"No. Chuck's checking with the airport. I put in a call to Henry Knight. He's on his way home. His very snotty secretary said she'll *try* to reach him and have him call us."

"She wouldn't give you his home number?" Star asked.

Paresi smiled. "I think she found me annoying."

Star gave him a look. "You think so?"

Paresi laughed. "Hey, I was a peach, but I could tell she thought I was too common to deal with Mr. Money, so she did what a good watchdog does, she threw a sandbag my way, but . . ."

He reached into the breast pocket of his pale blue shirt, and retrieved a scrap of paper.

"I got the number from the Newark PD. If he doesn't call me back, I'm going to enjoy surprising him in the middle of his dinner."

"And if he refuses to talk to you?"

Paresi's azure eyes twinkled. "I spoke to a Captain Bruno Castelliano, and he said if I have any trouble, he'll be more than happy to give Mr. Big a police escort to the nearest phone."

Star laughed. "I love you."

"I know." Paresi linked his arm through hers. "Come with me." He led her around the corner, toward the anteroom off the interrogation room.

"Where are we going?"

"To listen." Paresi opened the door.

"We don't have to do that; he's with Mitchell. Let them have some privacy."

"Chuck says the guy's a jerk. I think we should hear what he's got to say."

"But he's talking to Mitchell."

"So? Does that mean you're going to lay down on this?" Paresi said.

"What are you talking about?"

He jerked his thumb toward the one-way glass. "Him. Dan Rayner. Because he's a rich guy and Mitch's friend, are you going easy?"

Star put her hands on her hips. "*What?*"

"Ordinarily you wouldn't even *let* somebody in the room, let alone leave them there. You'd make them talk in front of you."

"Wait a minute," Star said defensively. "I'm not going soft, I just think he deserves some privacy. Besides, I trust Mitchell. If this guy says anything, he'll tell us."

Paresi folded his arms across his chest. "I trust Mitch, too, *but* this *jimoke* just may have killed his wife."

Star looked at her partner. They stared in silence at one another for a few seconds, then she crossed the floor and turned up the volume knob, allowing the conversation in the interrogation room to be heard.

"How you holding up, Danny?" Mitch asked his friend.

Dan Rayner's eyes filled with tears and he reached out for Mitch.

The doctor held him, letting him sob.

"Did she suffer? Did she die quickly?" He looked at Mitch, his face contorted, tears rained down his cheeks. "Tell me she died without pain."

Mitch wished he could, but even the prelim said that Cynthia Rayner died in agony. He closed his eyes, seeing her bruised and battered body on the steel table.

"I can't say yet, Danny," Mitch said. "I won't know until I've completed the autopsy."

He reached into his inside breast pocket. "I took these off of her. I thought you'd like to have them." He handed his friend a small brown envelope.

Dan Rayner emptied the contents into his palm: Cynthia Rayner's diamond stud earrings and plain gold wedding band. He clutched them in his fist. The sound of his anguished weeping filled both the interrogation and the anteroom.

Mitch again took his sobbing friend into his arms, and looked directly at the "mirror" on the wall opposite them. He knew someone was on the other side, watching and listening. He also knew it was Star. He could *feel* her.

She saw the look on his face, and for the first time,

she felt apprehension. She knew from his eyes that Mitch would go to the mat for his friend.

Harlan Robinson dropped his coat on the bench at the door and headed straight for the liquor cabinet.

"Harlan?" his wife of eighteen years called out from the kitchen. "Harlan, is that you?"

"Who else would it be?" he muttered to himself. "Yeah, it's me," he called out.

Joyce Mitchell-Robinson walked into the study at the front of the house. She smiled at her husband. A quick, habitual grin that never reached her eyes.

"Dinner will be ready soon," she said, kissing him on the cheek.

Harlan sank down in the gray leather chair near the fireplace, his Jack Daniels splashed a bit, and the ice cubes bounced off the crystal walls of the glass, giving off a faint but merry tinkling sound.

He looked at his wife. She was standing there wearing jeans, a bright red polo shirt, and a navy blue chef's apron. She held a long meat fork in her hand.

Why did she insist on cooking dinner, on cleaning her own house? It didn't look good for a man of his success to have a wife whose fingernails were always unpainted and worn down from scrubbing and washing.

She'd tried early on in the marriage, when his

success was new, to be a society wife. She spent days at the spa being "pampered," but that had stopped years ago.

Joyce Robinson was most comfortable with hard work. She had grown up the eldest of two brothers and four sisters. She'd worked from the time she could remember and felt there was dignity in it. She'd begun working in her junior year of high school at a catalog warehouse. After high school she had no ambition for college, but she wanted to learn a skill that would support her, so she chose court reporting. She hung on to her job at the warehouse, to pay for her classes.

The mostly older women who worked with her at the warehouse derided her ambition. They laughed at her in the cafeteria, when she spent her lunch and break time poring over her notes and textbooks. It didn't matter. She knew what she wanted. She wasn't going to be somebody else's workhorse for the rest of her life.

Joyce's own personal motivation was Bertha Jean Wilson. Like Joyce, the woman had begun working at the warehouse when she was a teenager. Now, she was well into her fifties, and still doing the same job. She even wore the same stupid hairstyle, now dyed black to cover the gray. Whenever Joyce felt like giving up, she'd look at Bertha Jean Wilson.

She worked long hours and saved every penny she could, which wasn't easy. Her family's constant neediness had nearly capsized her career plans on more than one occasion, but she persevered. When she graduated and became a court reporter, her mother gave her an eighteen-carat-gold cross on a hammered gold chain.

She knew just how much Willadeen Mitchell had sacrificed for that gift. It became her most cherished possession, and she wore it around her neck to this day.

One of her first assignments after graduation had been Judge Robinson's court. Joyce was in love from the moment she saw him.

He noticed her right away. As she worked, their eyes would lock. The blush and innocence in hers made him smile. It didn't take long. Three dates, one sweaty all-nighter in which they did everything *but*, and he asked her to marry him. Her mother couldn't believe the fish she'd hooked. Willadeen Mitchell told her daughter to stay married "for keeps" no matter what it took.

In the beginning, that had been easy. They were in love, totally besotted with one another. But something happened to change all that.

Joyce became pregnant during their third year of marriage. Harlan was ecstatic, as was she. Then something went wrong. She lost the baby one snowy night, during one of the area's worst winter storms. She went into labor at the height of the blizzard, and it took far too long to get her to a hospital. Harlan's car refused to start, and when they finally got a taxi, the cab got stuck in the deep, heavy snow. Harlan himself had carried her, screaming in his arms, the remaining blocks to the hospital.

The baby was breech, and there were extreme complications. When Joyce awakened, her child was gone and her husband sat weeping at the foot of her bed. It was Harlan who told her their baby died and he authorized an emergency hysterectomy. It was the only way to stop the hemorrhaging, he explained. Her life depended on it.

Joyce wept so hard that she had to be sedated. From that time, nothing was ever the same between them. She felt like a husk of a woman. Whenever one of her sisters or her brother's wives brought forth a new life, she wanted to die. Her sadness etched itself into all the areas of her life with Harlan, until finally, she couldn't bear to have him touch her.

Her sister Bernice had tried talking to her about adoption, but Joyce didn't want to hear that. She didn't want somebody else's child, she wanted the impossible—her own flesh and blood. As the years passed, she went further and further into herself. Now, she and Harlan lived like brother and sister. It had been years since they'd made love.

Joyce wasn't stupid; she knew her husband saw other women. It was okay, as long as he was discreet, and came home to her. She never thought she'd lose him to anyone. Her friends were understanding to her face, but behind her back they thought she was insane, allowing him to bed other women and then come back to her.

She didn't care, she still loved him, but she honestly felt she had nothing to share, nothing to give to him as a woman. Years of therapy had done little to change her view. In time, they stopped the couple's counseling, and she stopped seeing her psychiatrist.

Joyce's house and her possessions became her life. She banished the housekeeper and cook, and took on all the duties herself. It gave her a feeling of peace to know that even if she couldn't give him a child, or physical love, she could give Harlan a clean, beautifully decorated home, wonderful meals, and be a perfect companion.

She looked at him slumped in the chair, his still handsome face sad and downturned. She knew he was hurting about something, but she didn't feel it her place to ask him.

"Dinner in fifteen minutes," she said, cheerier than she intended. Her husband didn't look up. His dark eyes studied the pattern in the lush burgundy carpet beneath his feet.

Joyce turned and walked from the room. If she kept quiet, maybe sooner or later, he'd tell her what was on his mind.

After his wife left, Harlan Robinson began to weep. Endless tears poured down his face.

His nose ran, his hands shook.

The amber liquid in his Steuben crystal glass splashed over the rim and onto his fingers.

He dropped it as if he'd been burned and buried his sobbing face in his hands. "Cyn," he whispered. "Cyn."

CHAPTER FIVE

The women's lockup was on the first floor of the Seventeenth Precinct. It sat at the end of a long hallway, just off the marble-floored main lobby.

The winding narrow path snaked past the communications room, two civilian workers' offices, a men's room, a women's room, and a perpetually locked door that no one could remember ever having seen open. It smelled of dirty bodies, Lysol, and despair.

The hallway served as the main path for transporting arrests from the lockup to the front desk. Once bail was made, or their custodial time was up, it was along this road that the precinct's overnight guests trudged. At the massive marble front desk, their belongings were returned, or they were just signed out from the drunk tank. This task was usually handled by elderly cops who'd made their bones on the street, and who now worked inside, counting the days till retirement.

Once past the women's room and the mystery

door, the hall branched out in three directions. To the right were the stairs leading down to the men's lockup.

The old marble steps were worn smooth from years of traffic. The black wrought-iron bannister showed patches of rust on its surface and in some of the ornate carvings that anchored it to the steps.

The Seventeenth was housed in one of the oldest buildings in the city. In fact, it had been declared a landmark, which made it immune to demolition. Its size and faded glory also made the financial reality of renovation something that the city government was perpetually "getting to."

All of this combined to greatly distress those who worked there.

To the left sat an ancient elevator, which was mostly used to ferry contraband and equipment to the property and supply rooms located in the basement. The secured area was once one big space, but during the Great Depression, it was split into two rooms. A doorway that allowed access to either room without having to exit to the hallway, was installed in the 1950s.

One room held inventoried evidence and the other contained surplus ammunition, tear gas, nightsticks and such.

Past the elevator, straight ahead, at the end of the hall, was a large, scarred heavy steel door that clanged shut with such finality that it always gave Star the willies. Behind it was the women's lockup.

Star shifted the paper bag she carried to her left hand and pushed the buzzer.

The matron answered instantly, her voice tinny over the intercom.

"Yes?"

Star leaned close to the microphone. "Hi, Carol, it's me, Star Duvall."

The buzzer sounded again and Star pulled the metal handle. As she walked down the dismal, narrow hallway, the massive door clanged shut. Her shoulders involuntarily shivered and rose slightly.

She rounded the corner at the end of the hall, directly into a small, comfortable, well-lit office.

"Hi, Carol."

"Hey, Star."

Carol Schiller had been the night matron at the Seventeenth for as long as Star could remember. She was even there when Star was a young girl, during the days when her father, Sergeant Lenard Duvall, had been in uniform.

Carol's hair had gone from Lucille Ball red to white, but her clear blue eyes and deep dimpled child's smile were still intact.

"How's it going this morning?" Star asked.

"Oh, just fine." Carol looked at the clock over her desk. "Most of the house is already in court, and I'll be off in an hour, home in fifteen minutes, and in my bed in twenty."

"Sounds like a plan." Star smiled.

Carol nodded. "I guess you're here to see Ernestine Henderson, right?"

"Yep." Star lifted the brown paper bag in her hand. "I bought her some breakfast. Do you want to inspect this?"

Carol shook her head. "I trust you. What did you bring?"

"Nothing special, just cinnamon rolls and coffee," she said.

"That's nice. I'm sure she'll appreciate it. Rolls and fresh coffee certainly sound better than the dishwater, powdered eggs, and stale bread provided by the Commonwealth."

"Amen to that," Star said. "How's she doing?"

Carol's lips turned down at the corners. "She's been fine all night, just a little crying." She leaned close to Star. "But between you and me, I think she's sorry now, you know."

"Did she say that?"

Carol shook her head. "Not exactly. We talked some last night, and she just kept saying that she wished it could have been different."

Carol lowered her voice. "I didn't quite know how to respond. It's hard when it's one of *the family*, no matter what a jerk he was."

"I know," Star said. "Willis had a rep, that's for sure. Still, he *was* one of our own, and in spite of the way he died, he's going to be given all the pomp and ceremony that goes with being a fallen cop."

Carol nodded. "I know that's tradition, but . . ."

"I hear you," Star said. "It gets me, too." She sighed. "My dad fell in the line of duty, and at the time, all of the ceremony helped, you know?"

"Your father was a wonderful man, Star," Carol said. "Even now, I think of him. His death was a sincere loss, but he died a hero. All of the ceremony for him was earned and deserved."

Star touched Carol's hand. "Thank you. That's how I feel." She looked toward the closed door that led to the cells.

"Her husband was a wife beater, and in my eyes, that's lower than snail shit. Still, he's going to get the same honors that my father got." She shook her head. "It pisses me off, Carol; I'm not sure I can even go to the funeral."

Carol put an arm around Star's shoulders.

"You listen to me. Your father was a hero, and always will be. And if he were here, he'd be the first one to tell you that what's done is done, and despite his human failings, Willis was *still* a police officer.

"So you suit up in your dress blues and be there to honor Len Duvall, because that's what he would have done. He would be there, to honor and salute the fallen cop, *not* the asshole husband."

"You're right," Star said. "You're absolutely right. Pop would have gone." She looked at the door again. "What's done is done, so we bury the bastard and take care of Ernestine. She's the one who needs help."

Carol gave her a little squeeze. "That's my girl." She picked up the cell keys from a hook hanging on the wall, near her small television. "She said he beat her senseless sometimes." She looked at Star, her blue eyes cloudy. "My first husband liked to hit me, too."

"How did you handle it?"

"I left. I took my two kids and walked." Carol indicated the door. "They didn't even have kids, so I don't know why she stayed. She should have just left him, because this is going to cost her the rest of her life."

"Maybe not," Star said. "Maybe not."

Cynthia Chapin-Rayner's naked and bruised body lay on the steel table.

Even though the day before, Mitch had performed the prelims and even X-rayed the body himself, the sight still broke his heart.

He stood alone in the cool, blue-tiled room, look-ing down at her. Dead eyes gazed back; the black-ness of her dilated pupils had nearly replaced the once clear blue of her eyes.

Mitch went to the compact CD player sitting on a shelf near the door, and rifled through a stack of CDs. He choose three, put them in the machine and hit the play button. James Taylor's *Hourglass* began. The singer's mellow voice filled the sterile room.

Mitch crossed to the sink, washed his hands, and dried them on a paper towel. He listened for a mo-ment to James singing about Richard Nixon, and then took a pair of latex gloves from the box over the sink and pulled them on.

He went back to the body.

"I remember how much you loved JT," he said. "Me, too. He always makes me feel better."

He leaned over, studying her dead face. "There's some Eric Clapton coming next," he said softly. "Remember that night, a million years ago, down on Boylston street when you, Danny, and I thought we saw him at Paul's Mall?" He smiled at the recollection.

"It was Mose Allison's show, remember? You said it had to be him, because you'd heard he was a big Mose Allison fan."

The happiness of the memory warmed him.

"While Danny and I were 'it is, it isn't,' you went right up and asked him." He chuckled. "Turns out he was just some guy from San Francisco, but he really did look like 'Slowhand.' "

Mitch gently touched Cynthia's face with his gloved fingers. Strands of blond hair, matted with dried blood, clung to her cheek. He carefully and tenderly moved it back. Though several deep wounds were visible on her scalp, X rays had revealed the depth of the damage to her skull. He'd still have to shave portions of her thick, curly mane to expose, measure, and document the damage the killer had inflicted on her.

Sadness clouded him. He blinked back tears.

"Oh, Cyn," Mitch whispered. "Who could have imagined this?"

His mind went back to the first day he'd met her.

Dan had shown up at Hanrahan's, a pub near the Harvard campus, with this tall, willowy, beautifully sunny creature holding his hand. Mitch liked her instantly. She was wild and funny, with a ribald, raucous sense of humor that never failed to send him into deep laughter. Indeed, he'd been so drawn to Cynthia that if Dan hadn't been his friend, he would have gone after her himself.

He tenderly turned her head.

"Who could do this to you?"

He traced a huge purple bruise that spread from her right breast, upward to her neck, and over her shoulder. His memory took him back to the day he was best man at her wedding to Dan.

"You were a piece of work," he said. "Leave it to you to shock the hell out of all of that old money."

Dan Rayner and Cynthia Chapin had been married in Newport, in a tiny church on the estate of one of Dan's father's business partners. On that day, Cynthia Chapin took Mitch's breath away. She was, at that moment, the most beautiful woman he'd ever seen.

Mitch remembered the audible gasp when the bride appeared in the doorway of the small chapel. Her hair was piled atop her head, momentarily tamed by a band of white baby roses. She looked like a Botticelli angel.

In her hand, she carried a bouquet of white roses and Stargazer lilies. But it was her decidedly un-demure, un-virginal wedding dress that floored the guests. It was a long, white, clingy, satin gown, seemingly worn without benefit of undergarments. The slinky dress was anchored front to back, over one bare shoulder with a starburst diamond brooch big enough to buy the entire state of Rhode Island.

She caught Mitch's stare and grinned at him.

With a toss of her head that dislodged a couple of her curls, Cynthia linked arms with her mother and began her glide down the aisle.

To say that she shocked the congregation would be mild. Her decision to be given away by her wealthy, but divorced mother had caused weeks of discussion among the WASPy sailing set before the wedding, and now this.

Mitch almost laughed, remembering the look on Dan's face. "Positively dumbstruck," he whispered. "And then you winked at me. You were amazing. The real deal, a genuine free spirit."

A tear slid down his cheek. "You were the best thing to ever happen to Dan, and exactly what those old coots needed to juice them up. They're still talking about that dress, and you in it."

He touched her face. "I'm going to miss you, Cyn."

"How are you this morning, Ernestine?" Star asked, as Carol unlocked the cell door.

Ernestine Henderson sat up on her bunk, and smiled. "I'm good, Lieutenant," she said, indicating a spot alongside her. "Come sit down."

Star went in and sat beside her. "I brought you some breakfast." She handed the woman the bag.

"Mmmmmm, this smells wonderful." Ernestine opened it and looked inside. "Ooh, I love fresh cinnamon buns, how did you know?"

Star shrugged. "Who doesn't?"

"Won't you have one?" Ernestine said.

"No, thank you." Star smiled. "I have *no* self control, I had two before I got here."

Ernestine turned toward Carol, who was standing at the cell door. "Mrs. Schiller, would you like a warm roll?"

"No, thanks," Carol said. "You go ahead, enjoy them."

"Oh, I will." Ernestine took a bite of the fragrant, sticky bun, a ribbon of warm, gooey icing settled on her bottom lip.

"There's coffee, too," Star said. "It's black." She pointed to the bag. "There's cream and sugar in there."

"Oh, thank you." Ernestine licked the frosting off her mouth and again reached into the bag.

"You're being arraigned this morning," Star said.

"Uh-huh. I know." The woman opened two of the little plastic cups of cream, and poured them into her coffee. "Mrs. Schiller said it's painless."

She smiled, and stirred the hot drink with a thin wooden stick from the bag.

"Do you know, all those years I was married to Willis, I never, ever set foot in a courtroom."

She inhaled the aroma from the disposable cup and sipped. "This is wonderful coffee," she said, smiling at the two women. "In fact, this is the best breakfast I've had in a long time." Star and Carol looked at each other.

Dan Rayner was sitting in Mitch's office when the doctor opened the door.

"Danny."

He stood, his colorless eyes reddened from tears and sleeplessness.

"Hi . . . your secretary let me in."

"That's fine." Mitch embraced his old friend.

"I want to see my wife."

Mitch indicated the sofa, and Dan sat down.

"I don't advise that, Danny. It's better if you wait."

Dan Rayner's eyes filled with tears.

"You mean wait until the undertaker's had a chance to make her look human again."

"Dan . . ."

"I'm sorry," he said, tears slipping down his unshaven face. "I'm sorry, Mitch, but I can't get my mind around this."

He leaned forward, his hands clasped between

his knees. "I kept expecting her to be there last night. I got up and went through the house, looking for her, before I realized she was really gone."

"I understand," Mitch said.

"Tell me how she died."

"Danny . . ."

"No." Rayner raised his hand. "Tell me, and don't lie. Don't try to soften it. Tell me *how* she died, Mitch."

Mitch sighed deeply, and sat down on the edge of his desk, facing his friend. He folded his arms across his chest.

"She was bludgeoned."

"Bludgeoned? You mean hit over the head?" Dan's voice trembled. "Somebody beat her to death?"

"Yes," Mitch said. "I'm sorry."

"Tell me what happened, tell me everything."

"Dan . . ."

"I have a right to know, goddammit Mitch, *tell me*!"

Mitch took a deep breath. "She was beaten severely about the head and body. There were eight wounds to the scalp, with three of them causing deep fractures to the skull."

"No . . ."

"Danny, I . . ."

"Go on," his friend said. "Go on, I want to know."

Mitch ran a hand through his hair. "There was

blunt force trauma to her chest and abdomen. There were lacerations and bruises on her thighs, breasts, back, and legs."

"Was she raped?"

"No . . ." Mitch said. "No signs of that. But she sustained second-degree chemical burns to the backs of her calves and the soles of her feet."

Dan buried his face in his hands.

Mitch leaned forward, his hand on his sobbing friend's shoulder.

"Danny, I'm sorry about Cyn . . . and the baby."

Dan Rayner looked at him, his face wet, his nose running. "Baby?" he said, his voice soft in the quiet room.

"Yes," Mitch said. "Cyn was pregnant . . . at least sixteen weeks."

Dan Rayner leaned back against the couch cushions; the surprise in his eyes overtook the anguish on his face.

"Danny?" Mitch moved to the sofa, next to his friend, his hand on Rayner's back. "You knew she was pregnant, didn't you?"

Dan Rayner looked at his friend. "Not by me." His voice was a hoarse whisper. "I had a vasectomy eight years ago."

CHAPTER SIX

"Good morning." Star dropped her purse noisily into her bottom desk drawer.

"Morning." Paresi looked up. "You got *foongi* face. What's wrong?"

"*Foongi* face?" She almost laughed.

"Picklepuss," Paresi said. "What happened?"

She sat down. "I stopped off to see Ernestine Henderson."

"And . . . ?"

"And I'm worried." Star folded her arms on the desktop and leaned toward her partner. "She's being arraigned this morning, and she's acting as if she's going to sleepaway camp or something."

"Sounds like shock," Paresi said. "The full force of what she did hasn't hit her yet."

"I thought of that, but no . . . this is different."

"How?"

"She's happy," Star said, incredulously. "Or at least, she appears to be."

85

"Have they done the psych evaluation yet?" Paresi asked.

"Not until after the arraignment"—Star looked at her watch—"which should be happening along about now." She sat back in her chair. "I'm telling you Paresi, something's really wrong there."

"Star?"

She looked up to see Detective Richardson.

"Hi, Chuck, what've you got?"

He handed her a manila folder. "Crime scene photos, and my report on the Rayner killing."

"Thanks." She opened the file, and winced. "These are pretty bad."

"It's rough, alright." Richardson looked over her shoulder. "The autopsy should be sometime today. I want to go, but Grant's office doesn't have a time yet."

"I'll give him a call," Star said.

"Thanks."

"Anything else turn up?" she asked.

Richardson shook his head. "Nope, nothing other than that pool cleaner that Tommy Bell said had been used as a fire starter."

"Now that was something I never knew," Paresi said.

"Me, neither," Star said. "I had no idea that a pool cleaner could start a fire."

Richardson nodded. "I remember back when I was in school . . ."

"They had fire then?" Paresi said, with a straight face.

Star laughed.

"Yeah." Chuck smiled. "Everywhere but in Sicily."

They laughed.

"Anyway," Richardson continued, "in chem class, they used to haul out certain dry chemicals and put on a show. Some of them could cause a lot of damage if they were lit, but I never would've thought about a pool cleaner. . . ."

"Have you checked the pool supply houses?" Star asked.

"Tommy Bell's crew is on that," Chuck said. "He tells me those guys are so tight, they can break down the formula and maybe even get us a brand name."

"Great," Star said. "Then we'll have something to take to the suppliers, see who sells it in this area."

"Right."

"Thanks, Chuck."

Her phone rang.

"Excuse me." She picked it up. "Homicide, Lieutenant Duvall."

Paresi knew from the look on her face that it was Mitch.

"Hi . . ." Star said. "We were just talking about you. Chuck Richardson's here, he wants to know when Mrs. Rayner will post." She glanced at the detective. "Oh . . . okay, sure. Bye."

She hung up.

"What's happening?" Chuck asked.

"The post is done. He did it himself, early this morning." She handed him the manila folder. "He said he'll get the report over A.S.A.P."

"That was pretty fast," Paresi said, eyeing Star.

"I guess he just wanted to get it over with," she said, not looking at him.

"I can understand that." Chuck nodded. "Just imagine cutting into a friend."

"He's done it before," Star said.

"Yeah," Chuck agreed. "I know it's his job, but he was really upset at the scene."

Star looked at him. "Really?"

"Oh, yeah." Chuck folded his arms across his chest. "To tell the truth, I thought he was gonna lose it just before he asked me to call you."

"He's a very kind man," Star said, "I'm sure seeing an old friend like that was painful."

"You're right. I don't know how he does it."

Paresi leaned on his desk. "I still think it's odd that he didn't let anybody here know he was going to post her."

"He just wanted to get it done," Star said forcefully, still not looking at her partner. "You know, get as much information as quickly as he could. I'm sure the report will be thorough."

"That's for sure," Chuck agreed. "The doc never misses anything." He looked at his watch. "Well, since that's done, I'll go check out Maxine Waterman again. Maybe she'll have something else to bring to the party. Later, guys."

He walked away.

Paresi sat staring at Star, who seemed to be finding infinite interest in the giant rubber band ball on her desk. She snapped several bands on it, not looking at him.

"I'm not attacking him," Paresi said softly.

Star unearthed another jiggly elastic loop from beneath the mound of pens, unsharpened pencils and paper clips in the middle drawer of her desk, and wound it around the ball.

"I know," she said, fishing for more bands.

"Then why won't you look at me?"

Star put the ball down on her desk and finally faced her partner. "Because I don't like what I'm thinking . . . Mitchell just isn't like that."

"I feel like that, too," Paresi said, "but you gotta admit, it's not like him to cut the department out on a post."

"I know . . ." Star's voice trailed off. "I'm concerned."

"About?"

"The way this thing is working him." She rocked in her chair, her arms around herself. "He sounded really upset, like he'd been crying."

"She was a personal friend."

"Right," Star said. "He's grieving, I realize that. But he sounded like there's something else happening, too."

Her body shivered involuntarily. She looked at Paresi. "You don't really think he'd cover up for his friend, do you?

"No," she said, answering herself, before Paresi could speak. "He wouldn't . . . he just wouldn't. If Dan Rayner is involved in this, Mitchell wouldn't hide it from us. . . ." Her voice softened. "He wouldn't hide it from me."

Paresi leaned forward in his chair, concern for her visible on his face.

"Listen Star, you know how I feel about Mitch. I think he's a stand-up guy. I've always thought that, but he and this 'Hatchet' guy go way back."

"I know. I know," she said. "But I also know him. If Dan Rayner is involved, old friend or no old friend, Mitchell wouldn't stand in the way of justice."

She looked at Paresi. "He just wouldn't."

CHAPTER SEVEN

Star and Mitch lay together on his sofa in front of the fireplace. The remnants of their take-out meal from China Garden sat on the coffee table, next to two empty plum wine bottles.

The silken sax of the late Grover Washington, Jr., flowed from the Bose sound system.

Mitch lay on his back with his eyes closed, his arm around her.

Star lay on her side, her head on his chest. Their long blue-jeaned legs entwined and their bare feet softly caressed one another's.

As Grover's sax gave way to Bill Withers singing "Just the Two of Us," he pulled her closer.

Star opened her eyes, raised her head, and looked at him.

Even in the combined softness of the fire and candlelight, she could see the tension on his face.

Her earlier conversation with Paresi came back.

He's not hiding anything. If Dan Rayner were

involved in this in any way, and he knew it, he
would tell me. Mitchell would tell me.

She lay back, nestling against him, listening to
him breathe. The steady rise and fall of his chest
comforted her.

She inhaled him.

The subtle scent of Acqua di Giò, by Giorgio Armani, his latest "favorite" cologne, both warmed
and contented her.

A man who smelled this much like heaven would
never lie to her. She raised her head and kissed
his neck, inching up. Her lips touched his ear,
and she slowly exhaled a warm, gentle breath
into it.

He moaned, and she felt a tremor go through him.

With his eyes still closed, Mitch turned on the
sofa, pulling her against him, wrapping both arms
around her.

She kissed his mouth, and gently slipped one
hand beneath his black T-shirt.

Sighing at the feel of her warm palm and fingers
moving up his side, and across his back, Mitch
shifted her effortlessly beneath him.

His mouth covered hers.

He kissed her with a combination of gentleness
and fierceness, as if his only source of life flowed
from her lips and tongue.

The hunger of the kiss shocked and then inflamed
her. Something surrendered inside her soul. Her

doubts disappeared, and she returned the kiss, matching his passion and heat.

Suddenly, Mitch pulled away. Breathing hard, he sat up, and ran his hands through his hair. He looked at her lying there, and something appeared in his eyes. Something she couldn't name, something she'd never seen before.

Shaking, Star sat up alongside him and took his hand in hers.

"What's wrong?" she said, trying to get her breath back to normal. "What happened?"

Mitch didn't speak.

"Do you want to talk?" she asked tenderly.

Mitch tightened his grip on her. "I wish I could."

The fear and doubt came back, slamming into her chest like a fist.

"I'm sorry about Cynthia," she managed to say.

He didn't answer, but he raised her hand to his mouth and kissed it.

"It's so hard to lose someone you love," she said, tasting those words in her mouth.

He kissed her hand again and pulled her into his arms. Together, they lay back against the soft, leather cushions.

"This hurts so much," he said.

Star's chest tightened. She lay her head on his shoulder. "Talk to me," she said softly.

He hugged her tighter, and was silent, as if he were weighing his words. Finally, he spoke. "I've known both Cyn and Danny forever."

Mitch took a deep breath and slowly exhaled. "I admit in the past few years, we haven't been as close as we had been, but I knew they were there."

Star nodded against him. "How's he doing?"

Mitch slipped his hand beneath her shirt, needing to touch her, cherishing the warmth of her skin and the feeling it gave him.

"Not good. I'm afraid he's going to do something to himself."

Star sat up, looking in his eyes.

Mitch met her gaze, a sadness came over his face. "He didn't kill her, Star."

"I didn't say he did," she said, leaning against him.

They didn't speak for a few minutes.

"I have to tell you, though," she said, the cop in her overtaking the woman. "I am curious about him. He's such a slash-and-burn raider. I guess I find it hard to imagine that he has any kind of a heart. When Chuck and I talked to him, there was no mournfulness in him at all. In fact, he seemed more put out with having to answer a few questions than he was at the fact of his wife's death."

Mitch looked at her with such sadness that she instantly wished she could take back the words.

"He's a man whose wife was murdered, and murdered horribly . . . viciously," Mitch said. "And in spite of what you may think, he's suffering. People handle pain in different ways, Star. I know Dan. Believe me, he's grieving."

"I'm sorry," she said truthfully. "I don't mean to sound so cold. It's just that he was *so* unemotional when we spoke to him. There was nothing there until you came in."

"Are you saying he was putting on an act for me?"

"No . . ." Star sat up, looking at him. "At least, I don't think it was an act."

Mitch turned on the sofa, facing her, taking both her hands in his.

"Listen to me. I respect what you're saying, and I can even understand why you're saying it, but I've known Dan Rayner for over half my life. Yes, he's changed, but he's not capable of what you're thinking. He's damned close to killing himself, Star, and it's no act.

"You're right in what you think about his job. It's mean, and cutthroat. He hurts people. What he does is dirty and vicious, and he's very good at it, but still, he loved Cyn. I was there from the beginning. I *saw* how they were together."

"But that was a long time ago."

"I agree," Mitch said, "and I'm not saying the marriage was perfect, but once you love somebody like that, it never really dies."

"Is that the case with you and Carole Ann?" Star blurted, again wishing she could sew her lips shut.

"Carole Ann?" Mitch said. "Ah . . . I see, this is about my ex?"

"No." Star looked down at their entwined

hands. She shook her head. "I don't want to fight with you. I know you're hurting for your friend. I'm sorry."

He laced his fingers through hers. "It's okay."

"No, it's not," she said. "I'm behaving like an idiot." She gazed intently at him. "I'm just worried about you."

Mitch touched her face. "Don't be . . . I'll get through this."

"I can't help it," she said, her voice small and soft. "I hate seeing you in so much pain. I can't do anything to help you, and it makes me crazy."

He kissed her, gently, softly, and leaned his forehead against hers.

"This is one of the worst things I've ever had to do," he said.

She touched his face.

Mitch kissed the palm of her hand and held it against his cheek. "Danny asked me how she died," he whispered, "and I *lied* to him."

"Oh honey, that's understandable." Star made him look at her. "There's nothing wrong with lying about that. You just didn't want to tell him the clinical facts."

"No." Mitch shook his head. "I told him about her wounds, the blunt force trauma . . . I even told him she was pregnant."

"Pregnant?" Star's eyes widened.

Mitch nodded. "At least sixteen weeks."

"He didn't know?"

Mitch shook his head. "The baby wasn't his. Evidently, Cyn was having an affair."

She leaned back on the sofa, still holding his hand, trying to absorb this new information.

"If you told him all that, what did you leave out?"

Mitch turned to her; his grip on her hand tightened.

"What I didn't tell him . . . what I *couldn't* tell him, was that I found her panties stuffed down inside her throat, and a footprint on her neck."

Angelo Paresi hugged his nephew and kissed him on both cheeks. "So where you been? You forget you got a family?" Though he had lived in America for over sixty years, his voice still carried the trace of Sicilian sunrises.

"Hey, Uncle Ange." Paresi returned the hug.

Paresi's uncle affectionately ruffled his hair and turned to Vee. He pulled her into his arms. "Verenita." He kissed her on both cheeks. "How are the boys, and that beautiful little angel, Lena?"

"Everyone's well, Angelo. How are you?"

Angelo spread his hands in front of him, and then clasped them to his chest. "I'm an old man. Every day I wake up above ground is a good day." He patted Paresi's cheek. "Look at my boy here, he's happy, you must be taking good care of him."

"I'm doing my best." Vee smiled.

He kissed her again. "You're doing all the right things. I can see his heart . . . it's happy."

Paresi looked around the crowded restaurant.

"You got room for us, Uncle Ange? Looks like a pretty full house."

"I always got a place for *mi famiglia*." He helped Vee remove her coat. "So where's my other favorite couple?"

"Star and Mitch couldn't make it tonight." Paresi slipped out of his overcoat.

His uncle took it, laying it over his arm, on top of Vee's. "I hope everything's alright."

He beckoned a young curly haired waiter. "Luciano, hang these up in the office, and set up a table in the private dining room."

"Right away, Angelo." The young man nodded at them, took the coats, and disappeared toward the back of the restaurant.

Angelo put his arms around Vee and Paresi.

"Come on, have some vino, while he sets the room."

He walked them to the bar, and opened a rich Chianti Rufina.

Paresi looked at the label. "The good stuff, thanks, unc."

Angelo handed a glass to Vee and she sipped. "Mmmmmm. This *is* good."

Angelo smiled, and poured another glass. "The

Tuscans, they're barbarians, but they make excellent vino."

Paresi laughed.

"So where you been, hotshot?" Angelo handed him a glass of wine and poured another for himself.

"Just busy Unc, lots of stuff going down."

"I read in the paper that the wife of some rich guy was killed. That yours?"

Paresi sipped his wine. "Technically, it belongs to another detective, but Star and I've gotten involved."

"The papers say she was found in a pit, in the woods. That so?"

Paresi nodded. "Yes."

Angelo shook his head. "Sounds like the old days."

"What does that mean?" Paresi said. "You think it's a 'hit'?"

Angelo looked at Vee. "Listen to him. I tell him all his life, there's no such thing as *mafioso*, but he listens to the movies instead of his uncle."

Vee laughed.

"No, you *chooch*," Angelo said to his nephew. "I mean it sounds like a stoning. You know, back in the old days, if a woman was loose with her marriage vows and she got caught, she got stoned."

"Stoning," Paresi said. "In this day and age?"

Angelo nodded. "Yes. In some regions they still do it. The woman is loose, they shove her in a pit and hit her with rocks till she's dead."

"What about the man?" Vee asked.

"They let him go."

"Figures." She sipped her wine.

"But not always," Angelo said. "Sometimes they kill him, too."

The waiter walked up to the bar. "Your table is ready," he said to Paresi. "Follow me."

"*Gratzi,* Luciano," Angelo said. "I'll take them."

"*Prego.*" The waiter smiled, and handed Angelo two maroon, leather-bound menus. "Enjoy your dinner," he said to Vee and Paresi, and moved off.

"Take your wine," Angelo said. "I'll have the bottle brought to your table." They picked up their glasses and he walked them toward an arched doorway off the main dining area.

The room was small and intimate, away from the noisiness of the main dining room. The round table, set for two, boasted crisp white linens, beautiful china, and an arrangement of pale pink roses in the center.

"This is so lovely." Vee set her glass on the table.

"Thanks Uncle Ange." Paresi touched his uncle's face.

"Glad you like it." Angelo pulled out Vee's chair.

"Thank you." She sat down.

"*Prego, Belladonna.*" He turned to his nephew. "So Star and the doctor, you know what's happening?"

Paresi sat opposite Vee. He put his glass of wine

next to his plate. "That woman in the woods was married to a friend of Mitch's."

"The rich guy what goes around firing people?"

"Yeah, he and the doc are close."

Angelo waved a hand. "Nah! What would Mitch wanna know some *gagootz* like that, huh?"

"They went to school together, Uncle Ange. They've known each other for a long time."

Angelo shook his head. His silver hair gleamed in the soft light of the room. "I don't care. I can't see the doctor involved with a *chooch* that would take jobs away from decent people. No, not a guy like that."

"Well, they don't *hang out* together," Paresi said. "But Mitch is taking this killing pretty hard."

"Now *that* I believe," Angelo said. "He's got a big heart, and Star, she loves him, so I can see she'd take care of him."

"The funeral is tomorrow, so she's with him tonight," Vee said. "I talked to her earlier. Mitch is very upset."

"Well, you tell him I'm sorry for his loss," Angelo said, handing them their menus.

"I'm gonna have Rosa pack up a lasagna for him and Star. You can take it when you go. That way, they won't have to think about dinner. It will heat right up and taste even better tomorrow."

"Thanks, unc." Paresi stood up and hugged his father's brother.

"I'm gonna go tell your aunt Rosa you're here."

"Okay." Paresi kissed his uncle again.

Vee watched Angelo leave.

"I adore the way you are with your family."

Paresi watched his uncle until he disappeared.

"I love that old guy," he said. "My father died when I was eight, and Uncle Ange took over."

A tenderness crossed Paresi's face, his blue eyes glistened in the soft light. "He raised me and my sisters, and he's never, ever let me, or any one of us, down." His voice caught in his throat. "He's like a rock. Everything good in me, came from him."

Vee took his hand across the table. "He's a wonderful man," she said. "He always makes me and the kids feel like family. Although . . ." She raised an eyebrow.

"What?"

"He called me '*Belladonna*,' " she said. "Isn't that poison?"

Paresi laughed. "Yes, that's another name for Deadly Nightshade, a beautiful but dangerous plant; it also means 'beautiful lady.' " He kissed her hand. "My uncle likes beautiful women," Paresi said. "Pure and simple. He worships Aunt Rosa, but a pretty face to Angelo Paresi is a pretty face . . . no matter what color it is."

"Just like his nephew, huh?" Vee grinned.

"Absolutely!" Paresi laughed. "Who do you think taught me to appreciate beauty?"

Vee giggled.

"Seriously," Paresi said, "he's never had any prejudice. When he came to America, Uncle Ange worked alongside every kind of person here. All he saw was that they were all in the same boat, working for their families and their dreams.

"He fought in World War II, and saw combat with whites, blacks, hispanics . . . you name it. The only thing racial that upset him was that the troops were segregated.

"He used to tell us stories about his time in the war, and he said that the black soldiers bled red right along with everybody else.

"He said that FDR was a great man, but it was Truman that he respected, because Truman ended segregation of the troops.

"That old guy's pushing seventy-three," Paresi said, "and he's seen a lot of life. He judges people by one thing, and one thing only."

He put Vee's hand on his chest, over his heart. "What's in here. That's the only thing that counts with Angelo Paresi, and that's how he raised me, and my sisters."

"He's an amazing man," Vee said.

Paresi nodded. "You bet, and a smart one."

She looked at him.

"What he said . . ."

"What?"

"Stoning . . . that's something I never would have

thought of in a million years. Maybe Mrs. 'Hatchet' was involved with some guy other than her husband, and maybe somebody knew it and decided she should pay for it."

CHAPTER EIGHT

The church sat on a hilltop, nestled beneath a canopy of weeping willow trees. The driveway leading up to the arched stone facade was lined with luxury cars and black limousines. Mitch maneuvered his midnight blue Porsche around a Lincoln town car and parked. He got out, walked around the rear of the car, and opened the passenger door for Star.

He offered his hand, she took it, and got out. As they walked, still hand-in-hand, toward the chapel, Star was aware of the eyes on them, and of the faces, most of which she'd only seen on the pages of national news magazines and on television.

Beneath his gold-framed Fendi shades, Mitch's green eyes stared straight ahead. He knew most of the people crowding the vestibule of the church and spilling out into the morning sunshine, but he didn't feel like being polite or making small talk.

Inside the chapel, the fragrance of flowers was

both beautiful and overwhelming. Banks of blossoms covered the altar. A blanket of white roses lay atop the open white metal casket.

As Star and Mitch moved down the center aisle, she saw heads turning. At the casket, Mitch removed his sunglasses. His eyes were red and tired. They had talked through most of the night and then made love to the point of exhaustion. Still, he hadn't slept.

Star looked down at the woman in the coffin. The undertaker had indeed been a master of his art. Cynthia Chapin-Rayner looked as if she were peacefully sleeping. Still, Star knew that the white orchids entwined in her curly hair, the heavy pancake makeup on her face, and the beautiful white silk drape around her throat hid grievous wounds, bruises, and a footprint.

She squeezed Mitch's hand. "Are you going to be alright?"

"Yes," he said, his voice a hoarse whisper. "Let's sit down." He turned, still holding her hand, and led her toward a pew a few feet away from the altar.

As they sat down, Star looked up to see Dan Rayner coming through a side door of the chapel. He was alone. He walked slowly, with his head down, seemingly oblivious to the well-known faces viewing him with compassionate eyes. When he saw Mitch and Star, his face became alive.

"Mitch," he said, his voice surprisingly strong.

Dr. Grant stood and embraced him.

"I'm glad you came," Dan said, his eyes brimming.

Mitch indicated Star. "Dan, you know Lieutenant Duvall."

Dan Rayner's gaze was cold and dismissive, but his voice was polite. "Thank you for coming, detective."

Star didn't speak. She nodded and turned away, again facing the open casket.

"Come sit with me," Dan said to Mitch.

"Danny . . . your family . . ." Mitch started.

"You're my family, Mitch," he said. "You have been for a long time, even if you didn't know it."

Mitch turned to Star.

Dan extended his hand toward her, the coldness still in his eyes, but not his voice. "Please, both of you, come sit with me."

Star didn't like this man. She could see, even in his grief, that he would rather she *not* be with them, but he couldn't offend Mitch.

She stood, and they followed Dan Rayner to the front pew, just a few feet from the open casket. Star sat down, while Mitch accompanied his friend to the bier.

As she sat, trying not to stare at the celebrities on all sides of her, Star became aware that she was being scrutinized.

She turned to see an aristocratic-looking blonde woman wearing an elegant black Donna Karan suit and a large-brimmed black hat. The woman didn't flinch when Star met her gaze. They stared at one another until finally Star looked away. Mitch came back and sat next to her, taking her hand.

Dan Rayner stayed at the casket, his head bowed. From the movement of his back and shoulders, Star knew he was sobbing.

Ernestine Henderson sat in her cell, her eyes closed, her head bowed. She was praying. The day matron, unlike Carol, left the door leading to the cells open. From the office, she could hear the newscaster talking about Cynthia Chapin-Rayner.

Although she'd never met the woman, and though Dan Rayner was responsible for the cutback, that had she not been jailed, would have cost her the job she'd held for nearly fifteen years; Ernestine Henderson prayed sincerely for the poor woman's soul.

The service, though brief, was wrenching. Dan Rayner kissed his wife for the last time, and supported by Mitch, walked down the aisle, leaving the church. Star followed, with the mourners filing out behind her.

Outside, Mitch helped Dan into a limousine parked directly in front of the door. He turned to Star.

"Danny wants us to ride with him. We can leave my car, and come back for it later."

"No, you go ahead," she said. "I think he needs to be alone with you."

Mitch looked concerned, and walked her a few feet from the car. "Are you sure?"

"It's fine." She took his hand. "In fact, I think I'll just get a taxi, and go back to the station."

Mitch pulled his car keys from his overcoat pocket.

"Take my car. I'll call you later."

Star took the keys to the Porsche. "Alright, I'll talk to you soon." They kissed briefly. She looked back at the limo, now surrounded by the social elite.

"Tell him I'm sorry about his wife," she said to Mitch.

He kissed her again. "I will."

Star watched him go back to the car, mingling comfortably with the rich and famous. He looked back at her, sending a silent kiss, before getting into the limousine.

She turned and headed for the Porsche. As she approached it, she was surprised to see a woman standing in front of the driver's side door. It was the same elegant, but frosty looking blonde who'd stared her down inside the church.

"Excuse me," Star said.

The woman didn't budge.

"Excuse me," she repeated, "you're in my way."

"This isn't your car," the woman said.

"I beg your pardon?"

"I said, this isn't your car, and I'm not moving."

Star shifted her purse strap on her shoulder, a little smile crossed her lips. "Let me guess, you're . . ."

"Mrs. Mitchell Grant," Carole Ann said, "and you must be the *maid*."

"Swell," Star said. "Move."

Carole Ann folded her arms across her chest. "I'm waiting for my husband."

"Your *ex*-husband is in the limo with his friend, and I'm taking his car so that I can get back to work, so move or I'll move you."

"With what?" Carole Ann said. "What've you got, a gun?"

Star smiled. "And a badge! Now get out of my way, or you're under arrest."

"*Carole Ann!*" Mitch's voice came from behind her.

Star turned.

"What do you want?" Mitch said.

"I told you, I want you to take Robin." She regarded him with glacial blue eyes. "You haven't returned my calls."

Mitch stepped close to her, his face calm, his eyes invisible behind his Fendi shades. His voice was low and even.

"In case you haven't noticed, Danny's wife was murdered. It's a funeral, Carole Ann, this is not the place."

In the face of his cool rage, his ex-wife yielded. "I thought I'd be able to see you, to sit with you and

Dan." She glanced at Star, renewing her anger. "I didn't realize you were bringing the help."

"Puh-leeze," Star said.

Mitch took his ex by the arm, moving her away from his car.

"I don't want a scene. Danny's in agony. I didn't even know you were here until I saw you harassing Star."

Carole Ann shot a contemptuous look over her shoulder.

"Star? What kind of name is that? Is she a lap dancer on the side?"

"I'll see you later," Star said to Mitch, unlocking his car door.

"Wait." He went to her. "I'm sorry, I didn't even know she was here."

"It's okay, it's not your fault. I'll talk to you later . . ." she looked at Carole Ann, *"at home."* She kissed him again, briefly, and got into the car.

"Is this one living with you?" Carole Ann said coldly.

"My living arrangements are none of your business." Mitch took her arm. "Come with me."

As Star drove down the path, away from the church, she looked into the rearview mirror and saw Mitch wrangling his ex toward the limousine that held Dan Rayner.

CHAPTER NINE

Vee was surprised to see her lifelong best friend show up at her office. In all the years she'd worked at Michaels, Soto and Associates, she could count on one hand, the visits she'd had from Star. Their schedules usually didn't allow them to see one another during the day. As Star walked into the office, Vee glanced at the clock on her desk. It was nearly noon, time for lunch. One look at Star's face, and she knew it would be a long one. Luckily her boss was understanding.

Fifteen minutes later, they were seated in a booth at Jessie Mae's, listening to Jimmy Reed singing "Bright Lights and Big City," while sharing a plate of "Cajun popcorn" and waiting for two steaming bowls of gumbo.

"When I saw you roll up in that Porsche, looking like Darth Vader instead of profilin', I knew something was up," Vee said, popping one of the tiny, spicy fried shrimp into her mouth.

"I'm telling you, Vee, if it hadn't been a funeral, I

would have had to arrest myself for kicking the hell out of that woman," Star said. "That's some flaming nerve, *ambushing* me at the car!"

On the box, Jimmy Reed faded into Z. Z. Hill, singing "Down Home Blues."

Vee ate another shrimp. "Well, technically, she wasn't waiting for you, she was waiting for Mitch. He's the one she wanted to ambush."

Star picked up a shrimp. "I guess, but what was she thinking? This was not the time or the place for crap like that." She put it in her mouth.

"She wasn't thinking at all," Vee said, wiping her fingers on a yellow paper napkin. "You walked in with her man, and believe me, that's all she could see."

"He's not *her* man," Star said, reaching for another shrimp. "They've been divorced since the year one, and she knows he's been with other women."

"That's true. *But,*" Vee raised her eyebrows, "he ain't never been with one that she could call '*the help.*'" She picked up a shrimp. "I don't care if they got divorced before the earth cooled, ain't no way Blondie can handle him being with you, ya dust-bustin', lap-dancin' Hootchie Mama!"

They fell out laughing.

"It's a new century," Star said, "she should just get over it." She picked up another shrimp. "Now, she wants to send the 'almost grown' daughter to stay with him." She popped the shrimp into her mouth.

"Sounds to me like she wants to break y'all up," Vee said.

"Uh-uh." Star nodded, chewing. "But I got news for Missy Ann, that ain't happening." She swallowed her shrimp and took a sip from her Pepsi. "That heifer should just give it up, 'cause me and the man, honey, we solid, and that's the way it be."

"I heard that." Vee laughed, raising her hand. They slapped palms. "And I'm not going to say I told you so . . ."

"Yeah you are." Star grinned. "If you didn't, you'd explode, fly all around this restaurant, and land on some poor soul's chitlins with your eyes bugging out."

They laughed some more.

"Y'all are the laughinest girls . . ." Jessie Mae stood over them, holding a round aluminum tray. "Always was gigglers, the botha y'all, even when y'all was little." She put the tray on the table and set the thick, brown bowls of fragrant stew in front of them.

"Here you go darlins. This is my best gumbo. I get the Andouille sausage shipped in from N'awlins, and the crab and oysters come fresh off the boat this morning. Nothing but the best. Y'all enjoy it."

Star inhaled the spicy aroma. "Mmmmmm, this smells like heaven." She dipped a spoon into the thick richness.

"Miss Jessie, you are the only person on the

planet who can get me to eat okra." She smiled at the older woman.

"That's 'cause I know how to fix it," Jessie Mae said. "Now you girls eat it while it's hot. My gumbo is good for you."

"Yes ma'am," they said in unison.

"I'll get y'all some of my Cajun corn bread."

"I love that sweetbread." Vee blew on a spoonful of gumbo.

"I know." Jessie patted her affectionately on the shoulder. "I been feedin' it to y'all since y'all was both little bitty girls. It should be just about ready to come out the oven, nice and hot. I'll be right back."

Star watched her walk toward the kitchen.

"What would we do without her?"

"I don't even want to think about it," Vee said. "She's getting on, you know."

"As long as she can keep cooking, she'll keep living," Star said, blowing on the spoonful of gumbo she held. "This place is what keeps her going." She ate the stew. "Mmmmm-hmmm, this is good."

Star sipped from her ice-filled glass of Pepsi, and glanced at the muted TV, mounted on a pedestal over the counter. She saw a smiling photo of Cynthia Chapin-Rayner on the screen, behind the left shoulder of the noon news anchorman.

"Excuse me, Ollie Mae?" Star called out to a waitress. "Could you turn that up?"

The young woman reached for the remote, bringing up the sound, drowning out Albert King singing "Blues Power."

"Services were held this morning for Cynthia Chapin-Rayner, wife of self-titled 'corporate shark' Dan Rayner." The voice of the newsman filled the restaurant. "Here's Eileen Massucco, with the story."

"Hey!" Ollie Mae called out from the counter. "Star, that's you!"

Star and Vee watched as footage from the morning services rolled across the screen. There she was, walking hand-in-hand with Mitch toward the church's doors, while the reporter's voice-over filled in the details of the celebrity funeral.

"Lord, that man is fine!" Vee said.

"Excuse me?" Star said, a bemused smile on her face.

"Well he is!" Vee said. "You look good, too, honey, but he is *wearing* that coat." She looked at Star. "Versace or Armani?"

"Versace," Star said.

"Mmmph, mmmph, mmmph." Vee put the last shrimp in her mouth.

"And he's holding your hand, too." Jessie Mae set a plate of hot corn bread squares down in front of them.

"See, that's what I like about that man." She pointed at the TV screen. "He ain't one to do in the dark, what he won't own in the light."

She turned, looking at Star. "I know it's a new

day, an' things is different for folks mixin', and all that, but there's still hateful, crazy people in this world, who don't like seeing that."

Again, Jessie faced the screen. "Now Dr. Grant, he a rich man, and that mean he can do what he want to," she said. "He don't have to put up with nothin' from nobody. Money guarantees you a big stick in this world. But even with all that, it still takes a real man to stand up in public, and say this is my woman, and not give a damn who thinks what."

She rested her hands on her hips. "I like him, Star, and I like him with you. He's a good man, hold on to him."

Star watched the images on the screen. "Yes ma'am," she said. "That's exactly what I'm going to do."

Paresi looked up when she sat down at her desk.

"Hey. I didn't expect you so soon."

"I didn't go to the cemetery. I went to lunch with Vee."

"Oh?" Paresi said. "She didn't tell me you two were meeting for lunch."

"She didn't know."

"Uh-oh," Paresi said. "What happened?"

Star leaned back in her chair. "Nothing that I want to talk about here."

"Okay." He rifled through the files on his desk. "This was waiting when I got in." He handed her two sheets of paper stapled together. "It's Chuck's finished report on his talk with the witness from the scene at Hamilton's Woods."

Star took the papers. "Mrs. Walker . . . Wal . . ."

"Waterman," Paresi said. "Maxine Waterman."

"Yeah, so, what did Mrs. Maxine Waterman have to say?"

Paresi stared at her.

"What?"

"I want you prepared for this one."

Star sat up straight. "Okay."

Paresi folded his arms and leaned on his desk.

"Mrs. Waterman claims that the other morning, when she found Mrs. 'Hatchet' in the pit, she also saw a black man running from that direction."

"She saw a black man running from the scene?"

"Not the scene," Paresi said, "the area. He was running in Hamilton's Woods, from the direction of where she found the body."

Star tilted her head. "Okay, I admit, that's unusual." She bent forward, her eyes searching Paresi's face.

"Now, was this the all-purpose, generic, scary black man, or did she have a description?"

"She did better than that," Paresi said.

"What? A name and phone number?" Star asked sarcastically.

"A name . . . and just wait till you hear it."

"I'm listening."

"Harlan . . . Dubois . . . Robinson," Paresi said slowly.

Star's eyes widened. "She saw Judge Robinson running from the scene?"

"One more time," Paresi said. "Running from the *direction* of the scene." He sat back. "In fact, that's what made her go that way. She said she'd never ventured through to the other side of the woods, and when she saw him running, she decided to check it out."

"And she's sure it was Judge Robinson?"

"She spoke to him."

"Spoke? Did he stop and have a conversation with her?"

"No, he kept running, but she did say good morning."

"How polite." Star swiveled in her seat. "So has anyone spoken to the judge regarding this?"

Paresi shook his head. "Nobody can find him. His calendar is empty until tomorrow morning. We've been calling all over town, even his wife doesn't know where he is."

Mitch sat in a deep maroon leather Queen Anne chair in the mahogany paneled den on the second floor of Dan Rayner's home. The three story, 12,000 square-foot house rested at the end of Hamilton's Woods, facing the forest.

From the window, through the white sheer curtains, he watched the last rays of the sun being absorbed by the thickness of the trees. The late afternoon sky turned a darkening pewter gray.

In the distance, through the nearly naked trees, Mitch could almost see the spot where Cynthia Rayner's body had been found. He felt his chest tighten.

Unable to shake one more hand, or gaze into any more sad eyes, he had left the downstairs gathering of mourners and sycophants surrounding his friend, and come upstairs to call Star.

She answered on the second ring.

"Homicide, Lieutenant Duvall."

"Hi," he said softly.

"Hi." She turned her chair away from Paresi. "How's it going?"

"The house is full of faces, every one of which is expressing so much sorrow, that I was drowning. I needed to hear you."

Star lowered her voice, nearly whispering into the mouthpiece. "I'm here, whenever you need me."

Mitch closed his eyes.

A connecting silence passed between them.

He sighed.

"How's Mr. Rayner?"

"Barely conscious," Mitch said. "He was sedated this morning, and he's been drinking pretty heavily since we got back."

"I saw some of it on the news."

Mitch looked out of the window. "Yes, it's a big

deal. I just want it to be over." He was quiet again. "Star . . . ?"

"Yes?"

"I'm sorry about Carole Ann. I had no idea she was going to be there. I didn't expect her. She never really liked Cyn anyway," he said. "She was always jealous, always thinking something was going on between us."

"Some things never change," Star said.

Mitch was quiet for a moment. When he spoke, his voice was barely a whisper. "I'm sorry that she gave you such a hard time, you didn't deserve it."

"That's alright," Star said. "I'm a big girl, I can take it. Besides, it's not your fault she's unhappy."

Mitch closed his eyes, and massaged his right temple. "According to her it is."

"Did she go with you to the cemetery?"

"Yes. Actually she was good with Danny, so it turned out okay."

A knock on the door interrupted him.

"Hang on."

She heard him open the door, but she couldn't hear the conversation. In a moment, he was back.

"Star?"

"I'm here."

"I've got to go, Danny's asking for me."

"Is Carole Ann at the house?" Star blurted, instantly wishing she hadn't.

"Yes," Mitch said. "She's here, but we're keeping

our distance. I've got to go, I'll see you at my place, around seven?"

"I'll be there."

"I love you, baby," he said.

"Love you back." She hung up and turned to her partner.

"Sounds like you and the former Mrs. Doctor Grant met this morning," Paresi said. "Right?"

Star nodded. "And it wasn't pretty."

"What happened?"

"I'll tell you later," she said. "Right now, I'm wondering just where we might find Judge Robinson."

Harlan Robinson waited patiently for the cemetery workers to finish drawing the tarp and stacking the flowers over Cynthia Chapin-Rayner's still open grave. When the men left for lunch, he came out of his sanctuary. He'd watched the burial from a copse of ancient oaks on a rise overlooking the grave.

He was close enough to hear some of the minister's words, as she was laid to rest. He saw the celebrities and dignitaries surrounding Dan Rayner. He also saw Mitchell Grant.

Harlan had stepped farther back into the trees, because he expected Grant to be with Starletta Duvall, and he was sure she'd spot him. When he didn't see her, he ventured a bit out of his shelter.

There was a woman standing with Mitch Grant, but she definitely was not the lieutenant. In fact, he knew the elegant, classically dressed blonde was Carole Ann Grant, Mitch's former wife. He'd met her at several social events when she and Mitch were still married. Though she stood next to him, there was no contact. The chill between them was almost visible. Harlan knew she was just filling space.

Dan Rayner looked close to collapse, but Harlan didn't feel an ounce of sympathy for him. Dan had treated Cyn like dirt. Harlan's mind went to the times she cried in his arms, usually after making love. She would tell him how much he meant to her, how he was restoring her soul, after Dan had destroyed her.

She would enfold him, wrapping her long arms and legs around him, weeping as if she were breaking in two. He'd held her during those times, hating Dan Rayner more than anyone or anything on earth.

As the memories rushed over him, Harlan's hands curled into fists. He leaned against one of the great oaks, his eyes closed, waiting for the rage to pass, praying that he wouldn't break free from his hiding place and strangle Dan Rayner with his bare hands.

Finally, it was over. The last of the mourners left, and the workers broke for lunch. Now, he could say good-bye.

Harlan walked slowly down the small hill and to

the edge of the grave. The damp earth and the large bank of flowers gave off a sickly, sweet aroma.

He sank to his knees, feeling the chilly wetness of the grass being absorbed into the expensive fabric of his Vestamente suit, and into his cold flesh beneath.

He clasped his hands in front of him and bowed his head, but he couldn't cry. Not another tear, not anymore.

His eyes were painfully dry. His chest pounded with the irregular rhythm of his heart. He thought for a moment he was having a heart attack.

"Cyn," he said out loud. "Oh, baby, I'm so sorry."

The tears that he thought were dry, again started to flow. "I'm sorry," he said over and over, "I'm sorry."

CHAPTER TEN

"I saw you on the news last night," Chuck Richardson said, as he approached Star's desk.

"At six and eleven, they tell me." She sipped the latté Paresi had brought her that morning. "So, are you ready to go check out Judge Robinson?"

Chuck nodded. "I didn't know you'd be coming with me."

"It's your lucky day," she said, standing. "I've got an appointment with Dr. Grant later to discuss the autopsy, and I want you there. I figured we could go and check out the judge, then head over to the ME's office afterward."

"Okay."

"Paresi will meet us there. Right now, he's with Tommy Bell. There's been some ID on the pool cleaner."

Chuck put on his coat. His cinnamon-colored skin suddenly flushed. He looked at her, his face saddened and perplexed.

"I tell you Star, since I've been on this job, I've seen a lot of bad, nasty, and downright evil stuff, but to beat a woman to death, and then pour a caustic chemical on her, trying to set her on fire . . . that's beyond sick."

"It gets worse," Star said, remembering Mitch's disclosure of the footprint on Cynthia's neck and the panties in her throat.

"It can't."

"Trust me." She put on her coat and picked up her latté. They began walking toward the squad room double doors.

"It's just crazy," Chuck said. "What kinda bastard could do that to a woman?"

Star shouldered one of the double doors, pushing it open. "Let's just hope it's not Judge Robinson."

Harlan Robinson saw Star and Homicide Detective Chuck Richardson enter his courtroom. They sat in the rear, in the spectator seats, watching him.

He refused to be spooked. He glanced at them as nonchalantly as possible, and willed his attention back to the case in front of him.

The young man at the defendant's table had inadvertently caused the death of his friend during a robbery.

The two, drunk and stupid, had beaten another drunk at the bar they frequented and taken his meager week's wages.

Following their getaway, amidst all the hooting and hollering, they became aware that a police cruiser was in pursuit. Instead of pulling over, and making it easy on themselves, the two drunken young men decided to run for it.

During the high-speed chase through the Tyler Hill section of the city, the defendant's friend and accomplice became ill. Refusing to stop, the defendant told his friend to hang out of the window. The unfortunate and not terribly bright friend proceeded to do just that.

As they careened around a corner, the defendant lost control of his pickup and it jumped a curb. His friend, hanging out of the passenger-side window, vomiting, struck his head on a lamppost, and died instantly.

The truck crashed into two parked cars and a fire hydrant before coming to rest atop the water-gushing hydrant.

Now, in addition to Robbery, Driving Under the Influence, Reckless Driving, Destruction of Public Property, and numerous other charges, including resisting arrest; the defendant, Roy Jack Parker was facing involuntary manslaughter for the death of his friend, Jared "Jeeter" Winstead.

Parker appeared shell-shocked. He sat, staring straight ahead, with empty, watery blue eyes. The only sign of life he exhibited was to alternately fidget with his pale tattooed hands on the table, or to sigh deeply and wag his small, red-haired, buzz cut, head from side to side.

His attorney, a slightly overweight, damp newbie from the Public Defender's office, was about three hours out of law school, and scared to death of the formidable Judge Robinson. His client's blank look didn't instill confidence, either. Whenever the lawyer looked at Parker, a new sheen of sweat broke out on his forehead.

Judge Robinson, not hearing the testimony of the police officer on the stand next to the bench, glanced again at the two detectives in the rear of his courtroom.

When the prosecutor finished questioning the witness, the judge called for a two-hour recess. As the jury filed out, Star and Richardson approached the fence around the perimeter of the bench.

"Judge Robinson," Star said, "may we have a moment of your time?"

He looked in her direction but avoided her eyes.

"I have an appointment, Lieutenant," he said, gathering his paperwork.

"It'll just take a moment," Star persisted.

Harlan looked at the faces watching him. His clerk, bailiff, and the court reporter. "In my chambers," he said. "Just give me ten minutes."

"Thank you, your honor," Star said.

Mitch stood up at his desk and stretched. The pain in his low back made him wince. He carried all of his stress in his lower vertebrae, and in the past few days, he'd felt as if he needed to be in traction. He stretched again and looked at the antique gold clock on his desk. Star and Paresi should be in his office in an hour.

He sat back down, staring at the stack of manila file folders holding autopsy reports awaiting his reading and signature. The last thing he felt like doing was reviewing and signing off on a mountain of paperwork, but he reached for the top one—Willis Henderson.

He opened the file. A downed police officer was usually a case he took personally, but Willis had been brought in on the same morning that Cynthia had been found.

Mitch checked the top of the report to find out which of his staff performed the autopsy. "Rajak Rao," he muttered. "You were in good hands, Willis." Though Dr. Rao was his newest staff member, he was a gifted pathologist from Bombay.

Mitch rifled through the pages. He didn't feel like reading the report. He didn't feel like doing anything, except holding Star.

He looked again at his clock, and put Willis's file back atop the stack on the corner of his desk. "I can't do this right now," he said out loud. "Think I'll check on Danny." He reached for the phone.

* * *

Something was off with Judge Robinson, and Star could feel it. He answered her questions calmly, but never once did he look directly at her.

"Again, you were in the area of Hamilton's Woods on the morning in question?" she asked.

"Yes." He nodded, his eyes down. "I live very near the area, Lieutenant, and I often take my morning run through the woods. I don't recall seeing Mrs. . . ." He looked past her, training his eyes on the signed photograph of Thurgood Marshall on the wall behind her. "Mrs. . . . Witt, uh, Walter is it?"

"Waterman," Star said, watching him. "Maxine Waterman."

"Yes, Mrs. Waterman." Harlan brushed an invisible speck from his robe, which he was still wearing. "I don't remember seeing anyone that morning."

He focused on Chuck. "Of course I had no idea that such a horrible crime had been committed. If I'd only gone perhaps a few yards in another direction, I might have seen something, or someone."

He rested his hands on top of the desk. Star noted the way he stroked the gold wedding band on his left ring finger.

"I can only say that what happened to Mrs. Rayner is very sad and unfortunate." He twisted the ring. "I've met her several times at social events. Both my wife and I have spoken to her and her husband on numerous occasions. It's all very sad, especially when someone like that is taken."

Again, he twisted the thick, gold band. "She was so vibrant and alive," he said softly.

"I beg your pardon?" Star said.

Judge Robinson finally looked at those weird, spooky eyes. "I said, it's a shame."

"Yes it is," Star said. "A real tragedy."

Paresi and Belezorian reached Mitch's office a few minutes ahead of Star and Chuck. When they arrived, Lorraine aimed her phony smile at Star and directed them to the conference room on the third floor.

Chuck opened the door to find the doctor and the detectives studying a display of autopsy photos that had been arranged atop the long oak table.

"This is unbelievable," Paresi said, looking at a close-up of the angry, raw burn on Cynthia Chapin-Rayner's left rear calf.

"She was definitely alive when the chemical was poured," Mitch said softly.

Star moved alongside him, and looked at the photo. "She had to have felt this."

The doctor shook his head. "No. I'm pretty certain she was unconscious from the first blow." He pointed to a close-up photo of the side of Cynthia's pale face. "See that bruise?"

Star nodded.

"That's from a fist." He indicated his temple. "Here. She was punched, hard, which would have made her lose consciousness."

He picked up another photo. This one showed a shaven area of Cynthia's scalp. "Here, you can see the wounds. She was clubbed with enough force to fracture the skull. There's brain tissue leaking through in three places."

Star put her hand over her mouth.

"With being punched, and then having a blunt instrument strike the cranium, she went out, totally. The blows, though severe, didn't kill her, they just rendered her unconscious. She was alive when she was put in the pit. There were particles of dirt in her lower lateral cartilages, and in the passages."

"English, Doc," Belezorian said.

"Her nose, Tom. I found dirt from the pit in her nose. She'd inhaled enough of it for it to travel. It went into the passages and deep into her throat. That means she slumped, with her face in the dirt, or close enough to inhale the debris. She breathed it in for some time."

"But she was upright, her shoulders above the rim of the pit, when she was found, right?" Paresi asked.

"Yeah," Chuck said. "When we got there, she was slumped, but she was above the rim."

"She'd been arranged," Mitch said. "Her face had been in the dirt. There was dirt on her skin, her lips and tongue."

"That's weird. In cases like this, more often, the victim is gagged," Paresi said.

"She was." Mitch's face hardened. "She swallowed it." He plunged his hands into his pockets. Star watched the muscle in his jaw twitch. Instinctively, she touched his arm. He put one hand over hers.

"Estimating the time period between her being struck and put into the pit, as well as the severity of the chemical wounds," Mitch continued, "she had to have been alive when the chemical was dumped on her."

Chuck's eyes were furious. "Son of a bitch. How sick is this fuck?"

"You really want to know?" Mitch pointed to another gruesome close-up photograph. "This picture shows the prints on her throat."

"Prints?" Chuck said, looking over Mitch's shoulder. "Those aren't fingerprints."

"No," Mitch said. "They're shoe prints."

Chuck ran his hand over his mouth.

"I've already faxed copies of these photos to Loman Rayford in BCI," the doctor said. "He's running down the type of shoe, the manufacturer, and so forth." He pointed at the three reddish purple, arrow-shaped marks embedded in the pale flesh of Cynthia's throat.

"My guess is these are from some kind of athletic shoe."

"A running shoe?" Star asked.

Mitch looked at her. "Maybe."

"Are you saying somebody *stood* on her neck?" Chuck said, incredulously.

Mitch nodded. "Looks like it."

"And she swallowed the gag and choked," Paresi said.

Mitch's eyes glistened for a moment. "Her own panties. I found them inside her throat."

Chuck looked as if he were going to be sick.

"Whoever forced her underwear into her mouth would have no problem brutalizing her even more."

"Was she raped?" Star asked.

Mitch shook his head. "No. I did a kit, but there was nothing there, no sign of rape."

"What about the panties?"

"They're being analyzed," Mitch said. "We'll have the results in a couple of days."

Tommy reached into a folder near him.

"Well, I've got something on the mixture used to burn her." He handed Xeroxed copies of his report to each of them.

"The chemicals are an exclusive blend, made by the Neptune's Haven people. It's a special compound, and it comes in both liquid and crystal form." Belezorian handed out another copied sheet, showing the labels from both types of cleaner containers. "It's sold around here at Pool Que, Water World, and in the Village Discount Stores."

He pointed to the photos of Cynthia's burns. "Looks to me like the killer mixed the liquid and crystals for a more potent blend. That's why the burns are so severe. After she'd been doused, I think the rest of the compound was mixed and used as a fuse, to set her on fire. If it hadn't rained, it would've worked."

"And you actually think we're going to be able to find out who bought this stuff?" Chuck said. "Ain't gonna happen. There's about thirty Village Discount Stores throughout the Commonwealth, with at least a dozen in this area. We'd have to search the records for here and anyplace else within traveling distance."

"Never say never, my friend," Belezorian said. "We've got some serious bloodhounds in Arson. We don't quit."

"Glad to hear that, Tom," Mitch said. "This one's got to be solved. I don't think I can take it if whoever did this walks."

Star gently rested her hand on his lower back.

"I hear you, Doc," Belezorian said.

Paresi stood silently, gazing at a photo of Cynthia's body in the pit.

"You know, my Uncle Angelo said something the other night that's been rattling around in my head."

They looked at him.

"He said that in the old days, when a woman was committing adultery, you know, having an affair, she was punished by being stuck in a pit and hit with rocks until she died."

"Stoning," Mitch said.

Paresi nodded and picked up the photo. He turned the image of the brutalized woman in the pit toward the others. "Have you really looked at this?"

"Yes," Mitch said. "I have, and I admit, it's one of the first things I thought about when I saw her at the scene, but stoning is highly unlikely nowadays."

"Don't know about that, Doc," Paresi said. "Uncle Ange says it still goes on."

"In some parts of the world, I'm sure it does," Star said. "But in Brookport? Besides, she wasn't stoned to death, she was beaten with a blunt object, right?"

"Right," Mitch said. "But the beating wasn't the official cause of death."

"What then?" Paresi asked.

Mitch sighed deeply. "She actually suffocated. There was vomit in her lungs. She threw up from a combination of the weight on her neck and the panties in her throat. She aspirated."

Chuck shook his head.

"Still," Mitch said, taking the gruesome photo from Paresi's hand. "What you just said gives me pause, Dominic."

He looked at the detectives. "Danny dropped a little bomb on me the other day. He told me he's sterile, as a result of a vasectomy he had eight years ago, but . . ." Mitch wrestled with his emotions. "When Cyn died, she was sixteen weeks pregnant."

CHAPTER ELEVEN

Willis Henderson was laid to rest with all the pomp and ceremony given a fallen police officer. SWAT team members carried his bronze casket into and out of St. Michael's Church; officers from across the Commonwealth and beyond attended. The Mayor made a speech, as did Joseph Faraday, the Chief of Police. The media, out in force, crowded the old stone steps of the church, getting shots for the midday and evening news.

Inside, Star, in full uniform and white gloves, stood next to Paresi, also in dress blues. She leaned her shoulder against his.

"What?" he whispered.

"Across the aisle, about four pews back."

Paresi turned to look.

Judge Harlan Dubois Robinson stood across the vast middle aisle of St. Michael's with his head down, and his lips moving silently.

Paresi turned and looked at her, a questioning look in his azure eyes.

"Exactly," Star whispered. "Why is he here?"

Ernestine Henderson sat in the recreation area of the women's wing of the Mercer County Jail, watching her husband's funeral on TV.

Her eyes held a detached kind of curiosity as Willis's casket appeared, draped with an American flag. As it was borne from the church, by uniformed, white-gloved SWAT team members, Ernestine sat forward.

Behind the casket and pallbearers, came the mourners. She recognized Starletta Duvall, even in her uniform and hat. Behind her, she saw Captain Lewis, also in uniform, followed by a number of faces she couldn't identify. Her eyes strayed to the large numbered black-and-white clock on the wall over the television set.

"Ooh!" she said out loud, and reached for the remote. "I'm missing *General Hospital.*"

When Star and Paresi arrived back at the precinct, there was a message from Loman Rayford. They went directly to his office.

"Ooh-wee! Look at all that gold!" Loman said, as they walked in. He grinned at Star. "This is the first time I've ever seen you in full-dress uniform."

She did a small turn. "It's the department issue, stylin' black oxfords that make it, don't you think?"

She pointed to her shoes. "Note the authentic spit shine."

"Spit on 'em myself," Paresi said, closing the door.

"You ought to see this boy shine shoes." Star jerked her thumb toward Paresi. "Pops that rag like a pro."

She plopped down in a chair in front of Loman's desk and unbuttoned the top two gold engraved buttons from the shoulder of her double-breasted jacket. She folded the flap back against her collarbone. "This thing itches." She fixed Loman with a golden-eyed gaze. "Missed you this morning."

Paresi sat in a chair next to her.

"I had to be here," Loman said. "All this work got me excused." He pursed his full lips in a frown. "But for once I was glad to be overloaded. I never cared much for Willis Henderson. He used to get drunk and say things about women no man should ever even think, let alone say."

"Yeah, he was a prince," Paresi said, unbuttoning his uniform jacket. "Now I know why I hate serge." He scratched at his ribs.

"So, what have you got?" Star said.

Loman stood, rounded the desk, and sat on the edge, closer to the two officers. "I've got a report on the shoes, and the lab tells me that in addition to dirt and vomit, there was blood on the underpants in her throat."

"Hers?" Star asked.

"Don't know yet." He handed each of them a

report on the shoe print, and picked up two close-up photos of the shoe and the sole. He faced the pictures toward them, the one of the shoe on top.

"Okay." Loman picked up a grease pencil and used it as a pointer. "This is a running shoe, called Trailblazer. It's manufactured by The Boyden Company, which is part of a conglomerate called Health-Quest. Though Boyden is American based, the shoes are actually made in mainland China. The Trailblazer is their high-end runner. It comes in several styles, including a line for women. This one . . ." he pointed, "is a man's shoe."

Star handed the photo to Paresi.

"Can you tell the size?" he asked.

"Yep." Loman nodded. "It's a size twelve, and it's the best of the best, totally top of the line."

He held up the second photograph, showing the sole.

"Note the three arrows." He pointed. "Those little suckers make this model costlier than the others. This shoe retails for $239.99, and it's sold in this area only at Gilstrom's and at Good Sports, that yuppie sports equipment place in Mayfair Mall."

"What about knockoffs?" Star said.

Loman nodded. "We looked into that. There are some that look like this shoe at first glance, but if you check the sole, you'll see some of them have only one or two arrows and some have none."

Star looked at Paresi. "I guess we'd better get changed. We're going shopping."

Gilstrom's, located in the center of Brookport's historical downtown, was an elegant store. Slated for demolition in the boom economy of the eighties, the venerable business had been purchased by a coalition of European merchants who rescued both the store and its historic structure from the wrecking ball.

The gracious old building had been restored to its former glory. Each floor displayed original bronzed art deco moldings and light fixtures, cleaned and shined to gleaming brightness.

The front entry housed an authentic Thomas Hart Benton ceiling mural, which had been resurrected after spending decades under dirt and dust.

In addition to classic elegance, Gilstrom's also provided services no longer available in most department stores. The sales staff consisted of well-dressed, helpful, and trained personnel, ready to assist but not overwhelm.

Personal shoppers were available to all who asked, not just the rich and famous. Customer service was their cornerstone. Even in today's "who cares" market, Gilstrom's went the distance.

If you wanted an item they didn't have, or were out of (a rare occurrence, since the store had a large and scrupulously watched inventory), a salesperson would inquire as to where you could find it, and even call to make sure that what you wanted was available.

Its crowning touch was the elegant Gilstrom's Tea Room, located on the very top of the building. Floor-to-ceiling windows, draped in pale pink velvet, provided views of downtown Brookport, and the Atlantic Ocean beyond. Fresh flowers bloomed on every table. Uniformed waiters, pale pink linen table dressings, and a quartet playing classical music rounded out the sumptuous atmosphere.

Behind the enormous buffet, two white-uniformed and hatted chefs stood, courteously serving everything from perfectly rare prime rib to caviar on toast points with sour cream.

Waiters moved across the plush rose-colored carpet, pushing decadent dessert carts, offering cakes, pies, and sweet whipped-cream and chocolate-laden concoctions for which there were no words.

Champagne, as well as the finest teas and coffees, flowed freely.

Star and Paresi took the escalator to the sixth floor men's department, listening to the music floating down from the tearoom on the top floor.

"I love this store," she said, as they glided by elegant displays and clothing.

"It's nice," Paresi said. "When I was a kid, my uncle Ange bought my confirmation suit here."

"It's a great store," Star said. "Vee and I got our prom dresses here. We had this really nice older woman waiting on us." She laughed at the memory.

"Boy, was she a patient soul. We tried on practically every dress in the joint. Finally I ended up with a deep blue velvet gown, and Vee got this really pretty pink silk, strapless number." She grinned at Paresi. "Even then, she had something to hold it up."

He laughed. "I bet she was a knockout."

"Oh yeah." Star nodded. "She was a show-stopper."

They got onto the final escalator, leading to the men's department. The music from the tearoom floated down toward them. Star tilted her head, listening to Vivaldi's *Four Seasons*.

"Isn't that beautiful?" she said to Paresi. "When we were seniors, Vee and I saved for a month to have brunch at the tearoom."

"That must have been some meal."

Star laughed. "We heard they served champagne, so we figured that was our chance to try some. We got all dolled up, in high heels and makeup, trying to look older and sophisticated, but the waiters didn't offer any, and we were too chicken to ask."

"What gave you away?"

"I think it had something to do with me falling off my spiked heels with practically every step."

Laughing, they stepped off the escalator.

"Okay," she said as she turned, "men's shoes, there." They walked toward the section.

A young hispanic man wearing a well-fitted dark blue Prada suit and his dark hair in a ponytail, approached, smiling.

"Good afternoon, may I be of service?"

"Good afternoon." Star took her badge from her pocket. "I'm Lieutenant Duvall, Brookport PD, and this is my partner, Sergeant Paresi. We'd like to ask you a few questions about running shoes."

The young man looked nervous. "Yes ma'am, anything I can do to help."

"We're looking for a shoe called the Trailblazer."

"Oh yes, follow me." He led them toward a display of athletic shoes near the rear of the department.

"The Trailblazer is one of our best sellers." He stopped at a display. "As you can see, it comes in a variety of colors, with a range of models."

Paresi picked up one of the display shoes and turned it over.

"What's the difference?" He put the shoe down and picked up another one.

"Well," the salesman said. "This one . . ." he picked up the shoe Paresi had put down, "is the lower-priced model. It doesn't have the same amount of support in the arch, nor is it as lightweight as the top of the line shoe."

"May we see the top of the line?" Star asked.

"Certainly." He picked up another shoe. "This is absolutely the best model. It's so well-engineered that in spite of more arch support and padding, it's very lightweight." He turned the shoe around, showing the rear. "It also has a built-in light for nighttime safety." He pointed to a reflector light embedded in the heel.

"This shoe actually lights up?" Paresi said skeptically.

The young man nodded. "Uh-huh, there's a computer chip inside the shoe that senses darkness and automatically signals the light, which glows quite brightly at night. It's perfect for people who like to run at dusk or in the evening."

Paresi looked at Star.

"Could you turn that over?" she asked.

He turned the shoe upside down. The ridged underside of the shoe sported three deeply etched arrows in the sole.

"What do the arrows do?" Star asked.

The salesman smiled. "Nothing . . . they just look cool."

"Ah," Star said. "Do you keep a record of just who buys this top of the line shoe?"

"Well, we write up each sale."

"Cash and credit?" Star asked.

"Every sale rings through the computer, but the only ones that we can positively trace are check and charge sales."

"How far back do your records go?"

He put the shoe down. "At least five years. Do you have a particular date?"

"No," Star said, "but I have a size . . . twelve. Can you track down how many size twelve, top of the line Trailblazers you've sold in about, say a year?"

"Absolutely." He beckoned them. "Follow me."

* * *

Star put her hand over the fluted champagne glass on the table, as the waiter approached with a pink linen wrapped bottle of the bubbly wine.

"Sorry, no," she said.

He looked at Paresi.

"No, thanks."

The waiter smiled politely and moved to the next table.

Paresi watched him. "I don't believe I'm sitting here, turning down free champagne."

"I know." Star indicated the dessert in front of her. "As much as I'm loving this chocolate and whipped cream whatever it is, and this really fine coffee, it's not getting it. I can almost taste that champagne."

She looked around the room, at the elegantly appointed tables filled with mostly older women and a few men, some talking, most drinking.

"It was nice of the department manager to set us up to wait here, but we *are* on duty."

"I won't tell if you won't," Paresi said.

"Get thee behind me, Satan," Star whispered. "You know I love champagne."

He held up a finger. "How about just one glass?"

"We can't." She pointed at his dessert. "Just eat that strawberry thing . . . it looks good."

Paresi tilted his head. "It would go better with champagne."

"You really *are* the devil," she said, grinning.

He winked at her. "Wanna see my horns?"

They laughed.

"C'mon . . . how 'bout we split one glass?"

"Paresi . . ."

He could see she was weakening, but the arrival of the young, ponytailed salesman carrying a folder ended her temptation.

Captain Lewis looked at the printed computer records Star and Paresi had given him. He didn't say anything for a long time. Finally, he put the pages down and looked at his detectives.

"I guess there's no mistake here."

"None, Captain," Star said.

Lewis folded his arms across his chest. "It's going to be a bitch, getting a search warrant."

"I know," Star said. "Believe me, we checked it all out before we came to you." She pointed to the papers on his desk. "The store even provided a copy of the actual charge card receipt for the shoes. Everything's there, the account number, the name and signature, there's no mistake."

Lewis didn't say anything.

"I know nobody will want to touch it, Captain, but it has to be done."

Lewis frowned. "Richardson know about this?"

"Yessir," Star said. "We met with him when we got back from Gilstrom's. He's with Loman, taking a second look at the evidence."

"Okay." Lewis leaned forward in his chair. "Let

me make the call." He looked at his watch. "We'll get a warrant that covers the house and office."

"His club, too," Star said. "He plays golf a couple of times a week. He's got a locker there." She indicated the top sheet. "I wrote the name of it on the page."

"Right," Lewis said. "I see it. Anything else?"

"No sir," they said in unison.

"Okay, be ready to move first thing in the morning. We'll meet here, and get you some backup. Give Richardson the word."

"Thank you sir," Star said.

They walked toward the door.

"Detectives?" Lewis said.

Star and Paresi turned.

"Good work . . . both of you."

CHAPTER TWELVE

Mitch arrived at his penthouse apartment to find his ex-wife seated on the champagne-colored, silk brocade love seat in the hall outside his door.

"What are you doing here?"

"Nice to see you, too, darling." Carole Ann stood. "Chippendale or not, this thing is very uncomfortable." She picked up her coat and purse. "I tried using Robin's key, but it doesn't work."

"I had the locks changed," he said, opening the door.

"Are you planning to shut your daughter out, too?" She walked past him, into the apartment.

"Just you." He closed the door and went to the kitchen, setting the large white shopping bag he was carrying on the marble-topped center island.

"Why are you here, Carole Ann?" Mitch walked back toward the foyer, taking off his coat.

"We need to talk. I've been calling you for days and you still haven't bothered to return any of my messages."

He hung his coat in the antique French armoire near the door. "I told you at Cyn's funeral, I'm busy."

Carole Ann stood in the center of his living room. "Aren't you going to take my coat?" She held out the black, Donna Karan wrap.

"No," Mitch said. "You aren't staying."

Sighing, she dropped it and her Coach purse on the dark green leather sofa.

"Why?" She nodded toward the kitchen. "I see you've been to Movable Feast, that means gourmet takeout. I haven't had dinner yet, and judging from the size of the bag, there's enough for two." She folded her arms. "Think I've got what it takes to be a cop?"

"First you've got to be human." Mitch looked at his Rolex. "What you *have* is about three minutes."

"Then what? You're kicking me out?"

He walked back into the kitchen. His ex-wife followed.

"Robin will be coming home at the end of the month," she said. "I want her to come directly here. I don't want her at the house."

Mitch removed several white cartons from the bag and put them in the refrigerator. "You're amazing, you know that?"

"You finally noticed," she said.

He faced her.

"When we got divorced, I begged you for visitation

rights to my daughter, and you did everything you could to block them, including turning her against me."

"I had nothing to do with that. Your disgusting behavior is what made Robin loathe you."

Mitch walked out of the kitchen, she followed.

"You slept with anything that moved, and you didn't bother to hide it. How was she supposed to feel? How was she supposed to respect a father with the morals of a dog!"

Mitch picked up her coat from the sofa and threw it at her.

"Leave!"

"*No!*" Carole Ann threw it back at him. He let it fall to the floor. "We're having this out, and we're doing it *now*!"

Mitch moved close to her, stepping on her coat.

Carole Ann looked up at her ex-husband. She knew that glacial stare. She knew his anger. It was cold and hard. Where other men yelled, Mitch got very calm, and very dangerous.

She felt fear, mixed with a weird kind of excitement, creeping into her chest. She could still rattle his cage. A little smile appeared on her lips. She stood her ground, knowing he'd never hit her.

Mitch's eyes searched her face.

"You're enjoying this," he said. "That's typical of you, Carole Ann. Anger as an aphrodisiac. It's the only passion you respond to. You like it." His eyes locked on hers. "Better than sex, right?"

"You're perverted," she said, feeling the flush creeping through her body.

Mitch laughed. "I'm perverted? You're the one who uses sex as a bargaining chip. It's how you get what you want. It's how you got me to marry you."

"How dare you!"

"Don't . . ." he said, stepping closer.

Carole Ann could feel the electricity racing up her spine. Mitch was a very tall man, and her neck hurt from looking up, but she couldn't take her eyes off his.

"I was obsessed with you, and you used that. When I think back on it, it makes me sick."

"Mitch . . ."

"Don't say it. Don't even think it. Not that lie again. There was never any love, Carole Ann. It was all a plan to get me to the altar, and after the vows were said, you shut me out. All you wanted was money, power, and position, and I delivered."

Again, she opened her mouth.

"Not a word," Mitch said. "You shut yourself off from me, except for what . . . once every couple of months, and then you acted as if you were going to the guillotine rather than to bed. If you hadn't gotten drunk at the club, Robin wouldn't even be here."

"How can you . . ."

He raised his hand. "I said, not a word." His eyes darkened. "Yes, I cheated on you. There were lots of women, Carole Ann. They appreciated me. Some of them even loved me, but *none* of them were you.

"All I ever was to you was a bank account, a couple of houses, and a country club membership. Now, our daughter, whom you saw fit to poison against me, has evidently become her mother's child in every sense of the word, and you can't handle it. You can't stomach your own creation, can you?"

"I . . . I . . ." Carole Ann stuttered. The look on his face was beginning to really frighten her.

"Loo-cie, I'm home," Star called out, in a Desi Arnaz accented voice, from the foyer.

Mitch looked up. Carole Ann stepped back, her heart pounding.

"Hi, sweetie . . ." Star appeared in the living room doorway. "Oh, I'm sorry," she said, looking at Carole Ann's stricken face.

Mitch went to her and kissed her. "I'm glad you're here." He looked at his ex-wife. "Carole Ann is leaving."

"If you two have something to discuss . . ." Star looked from one to the other.

"The discussion is over," Mitch said, his eyes on Carole Ann. "I'll call Robin, and take care of everything."

Carole Ann picked up her coat and shook it, smoothing it with her hand. "Does she live here?"

"No, ma'am," Star said, "I jes cleans up and does a lil' lap-dancin' now and then."

Carole Ann grabbed her purse, blew past them, and slammed out of the penthouse apartment.

Star watched her go. "What the hell was that about?"

Joyce Robinson had just cleared the breakfast dishes and was getting ready to tidy the kitchen, when the front doorbell rang. She opened the door to find Starletta Duvall, Dominic Paresi, and four uniformed police officers on her doorstep.

"Mrs. Robinson?" Star said.

"Yes?" Joyce regarded them with a curious look.

"I'm Lieutenant Duvall, and this is my partner, Sergeant Paresi, Brookport PD, Homicide. . . ."

"Homicide?" Joyce interrupted, her eyes wide.

"Yes, ma'am." Star produced a document. "This is a search warrant; it gives us the authority to enter and search your home and property for evidence pertaining to the commission of a crime."

"What?" Joyce's face was ashen. "What are you talking about, what crime?"

"I know this is a shock, Mrs. Robinson, but we'll be in and out as quickly as we can, with as little damage as possible," Star said.

"I'm not letting you in here." Joyce tried to shut the door. Both Star and Paresi shouldered it, moving her back into the hallway.

"Ma'am," Star said, "I know this is difficult, but if you don't comply, we can and will arrest you for interfering with a police investigation."

"This is crazy, it's crazy." Joyce moved back from the door. Star and Paresi entered, followed by the uniformed officers.

"Thank you for your cooperation," Star said.

"You know what we're looking for," Paresi said to the officers. "You guys take the closets, and you two," he pointed to the second set, "check the garage and any outside buildings."

The four officers began moving.

"Mrs. Robinson," Star said, "I promise you, I will make this as painless as possible."

Joyce's eyes glistened with unshed tears. "May I call my husband?"

"Yes, ma'am."

She went toward the phone in the hall. Paresi moved next to Star.

"I almost hope we don't find anything here."

Star nodded. "I agree." She looked at him. "Let's get this over with."

"Judge Robinson's office."

"Verena?" Joyce Robinson's voice quivered, two tears rolled down her face.

"Mrs. Robinson?" Verena Rose, the judge's secretary said. "Is that you?"

"Yes," Joyce answered, crying now. "I need to speak to my husband, right away, it's an emergency."

"Just a moment."

Unable to reach him on the intercom, Verena got up and entered the judge's chambers. She tried not to see the blue uniformed officers tearing apart his wardrobe cabinet. His extra robes lay draped across the sofa, while they emptied every box and bag found in the chest.

Judge Robinson sat in his chair, watching, a sad, yet detached look in his eyes.

"Your honor?"

He looked up. "Yes, Verena?"

"I'm sorry, but your wife is on the phone. She's very upset."

Judge Robinson looked at Detective Richardson standing near his desk. "May I?"

Chuck nodded.

The judge picked up the phone. "Joyce?"

"Harlan, they're tearing the house apart."

"I know honey, I know."

"Lieutenant Duvall?" Star turned at the sound of the officer's voice.

"Can I see you outside?"

She looked at Paresi, and pointed to Joyce Robinson. "Stay with her."

"Okay."

She went out to the porch. "Did you find something?"

"Yes ma'am," the officer said. "In the garage."

Star followed him to the three-car garage. They entered through a side door from the yard. He led her to a doorless cabinet, with its contents in plain view.

"I know this isn't on the warrant, but I thought you should see it." He turned on a light near the cabinet.

"I read the report, you know, just to familiarize myself with what the case is about, and . . ." He pointed to the cabinet. "It *is* in plain sight."

Star plunged her hands in her pockets.

"You're right. Good work," she said. "Will you get Sergeant Paresi in here, please?"

"Yes, ma'am." The officer headed back to the house.

Star paced a little in front of the cabinet, not really wanting to see, but unable to avoid its contents.

"Judge Robinson," she whispered, "just what have you done?"

Harlan Dubois Robinson sat at the scarred green metal table in Interrogation Room Two, with a straight, almost military posture. He'd been sitting that way for nearly twenty minutes, his eyes staring straight ahead.

Richardson and Paresi sat opposite, both of them watching him. The only sound in the room was the muted breathing of the three men and the electronic ticking of the clock over the door.

In his office, Captain Lewis sat with Star.

"Where were the shoes?" he asked.

"One of the uniforms found them in the mudroom, just inside the back door."

"In plain view?"

Star nodded. "Yessir."

"Doesn't it seem to you, Lieutenant, that if a man killed somebody, wearing a pair of shoes that could bear evidence to his crime, wouldn't you think he'd get rid of them?"

Star sighed. "Captain Lewis, I feel as badly about this as anyone else. Granted, for whatever reason, Harlan Robinson and I don't get along, but all the evidence is here."

"The shoes were at his house and there were five bottles of Neptune's Haven Pool Cleaner in his garage."

"And an Olympic-sized pool in his backyard." The voice came from the doorway. Star and Lewis looked up.

"Afternoon." The short, white-haired man stepped into Lewis's office. "I'm Charles Sorensen, Judge Robinson's attorney. May I see my client?"

Both Star and Lewis stood.

"I'm Captain Lewis, and this is Lieutenant Duvall."

The man nodded at them. "From what I've been told, the evidence you've gathered on Judge Robinson is purely circumstantial." He adjusted his silk tie. "You do know that you won't be able to hold him."

Harlan Robinson saw his younger self on his bedroom TV screen. Old footage of his activist days in Brookport were being played, while a reporter droned over the picture about his arrest that morning on possible homicide charges in the death of Cynthia Chapin-Rayner.

At the mention of her name, the image on the screen switched to file footage of Cynthia and Dan Rayner arriving at some fundraiser or another.

She stood dutifully by his side as he was being interviewed, radiant in a bright red gown, with sparkling ruby butterflies nestled in her long, blond curls. Suddenly, she looked directly into the lens of the camera, and it seemed as if she were looking right into Harlan's soul.

He picked up the remote and turned off the television.

Somewhere from deep in the house, he could hear the sound of the vacuum. Joyce was still cleaning. She had not come down to the police station when he'd been taken in, and when he arrived home, she'd refused to speak to him.

She'd been polishing the furniture when he came in, and she hadn't even acknowledged his presence. Hours later, she was still cleaning.

Harlan lay back in his bed, his head throbbing, a

painful pulling sensation in his chest. The image of Cynthia Chapin-Rayner again appeared, this time, in his mind, and his heart. His eyes teared. He turned in his bed and shut off the light.

CHAPTER THIRTEEN

"That face is much too pretty to be looking so sad."

Star looked up. "Good morning, Loman. I hope you've got something to cheer me up."

Loman Rayford pulled up a chair next to her desk and settled himself into it.

"I heard about yesterday."

"It was horrible," Star said. "First, just to haul him in was bad enough, and then to watch him leave was worse."

Loman put a large hand on her shoulder. "You just did your job. He understands that. You had a reason to search, and you had a reason to bring him in. Nobody understands that better than Harlan. You serve the same law. We all do."

Star put her hand over his. "Thanks."

"Hey, Loman." Paresi set a cup of milky tea on the desk in front of Star.

"Thanks."

"Welcome." He sat down, stirring his cup of coffee.

"Where's mine?" Loman said.

"Over there," Paresi pointed toward the coffee-maker, "in the pot."

"No respect." Loman grinned. "No respect at all."

"I'll get you a cup of coffee, Loman," Star said.

"No, baby." He put his hand on her arm. "Hold off on that. I don't want nothing hot that you can throw at me. As a matter of fact, maybe we should move that tea."

Star leveled a gaze at him. "More bad news?"

"Just don't shoot the messenger," Loman said, opening the file folder he carried with him.

"Oh, boy," she muttered.

"The blood test on the panties, right?" Paresi asked.

"Right." Loman flipped through a couple of pages. "There is some good news."

The two detectives looked at him with anticipation.

"It's not hers. . . ."

"So . . ." they said in unison.

"So, it probably belongs to whoever killed her."

"You think she injured the killer?" Star asked.

"Possibly," Loman said. "Since the blood on the panties was not hers. There's a good chance she bit the guy, and he bled on the material."

"That *is* good news," Star said. "Have you got a type?"

"Yes," Loman said. "Yesterday, after the judge was brought in, I checked his medical records against the type on the panties."

"No match," Star said.

"Right." Loman closed the folder. "It's not his blood, but it's *somebody's* blood, and the tests show it's rare."

"How rare?" Paresi asked.

"AB."

"AB?" the detectives said in unison.

Loman nodded. "It's rare in both blacks and whites, but," he pointed to Star and himself, "we tend to have it more often. Data says about four percent of whites have AB blood, versus seven percent of blacks."

"So you think the killer is black?"

Loman shrugged. "Could be white, but the stain also showed a fragmented, dormant marking that could be sickle cell. We need more testing."

"Sickle cell definitely says black," Star said.

"What about DNA?" Paresi asked.

"That's the last resort," Loman said. "The cost is really high on that, and the city just might not do it."

"She was the wife of a rich man," Star said. "I guarantee you, there will be no complaint on getting DNA tests done."

"My, my, so cynical," Loman said. "Even if you're

right, which I'm sure you are, it'll take weeks at the very least to get results."

Star patted Loman's arm. "Well, at least it's something to look forward to. Thanks, it's a good break."

"I'll take that coffee now," he said, "and don't put sugar in it, just dip your little finger in there, that'll sweeten it up."

Star stood up, smiling. "Sugar Bear, I'm going to do you one better."

"Uh-oh," Loman said, grinning at Paresi.

"I'm taking you to lunch," Star said.

"I'm ready." The big man smiled.

"Tomorrow. I promise." She reached for her coat. "Right now, I'm going to the hearing for Ernestine Henderson. She's being sentenced today."

Ernestine Henderson turned in her seat when she heard the courtroom doors open. She beamed and waved as Starletta Duvall entered.

Star nodded and took a seat. The courtroom, except for the people who had to be there, was empty.

Star sat directly behind Ernestine and her attorney, a young, red-haired white woman, who kept admonishing her client to face the judge.

Ernestine was as excited as if she were about to be sent on a world cruise. She fidgeted at the table, like a six year old.

Judge Calvin Sumner ignored her as he slowly read the papers in front of him. He was about two years older than dirt, and given to actually falling asleep on the bench.

After what seemed an eternity, he looked up. His loose, red-veined, hanging jowls reminded Star of the sad-faced dogs in cartoons. His eyes, faded blue and watery behind his glasses, peered at her across the courtroom.

"Lieutenant Duvall, this is a closed sentencing." He sounded as if he were gargling marbles.

Star stood up. "I know, Your Honor. I'm here in my capacity as a police officer, to speak on behalf of the defendant."

He stared at her. "She pled guilty, there's nothing more to say."

"Yes, Your Honor," Star said. "I understand, but I have witnessed, firsthand, the abusive treatment the defendant received at the hands of her deceased husband. Perhaps if the court hears how severe the problem was, it will be more lenient and tolerant with her sentence. May I speak?"

He looked to the attorney. She looked to Ernestine, who had again turned in her seat, beaming at Star.

"We would welcome anything the officer could add, your honor," the attorney said.

"Very well." He looked at Star. "Come forward, Lieutenant."

"Thank you, sir." Star went to the witness stand. As she was being sworn in, Ernestine silently mouthed "Thank you."

* * *

Dan Rayner sat in Dr. Grant's office, a glassy stare in his eyes. His old friend could smell the whisky on him.

"I'm going back to work, Mitch," he said, his words slightly slurred. "I'm going to Chicago in the morning, there's a big baking company there, needs my help."

"Do you think you're ready to do that?"

Rayner nodded. "Yeah, I need to get back in the saddle." He looked at Mitch, his eyes red. "I just wanted to come by here and thank you for everything."

"No need, Danny."

Rayner looked out the window, and ran a hand over his mouth. Mitch noted the tremor in his fingers.

"I'm not going to lie and say this has been easy, but I've got to move on." He looked at Mitch. "If I stay around here, all I do is think about her. Getting back to work will be good for me." His face flushed. "Even with knowing she was pregnant by another man, I miss her." His eyes watered. "God help me, I still love her." A tear ran down his face. "I'm ashamed to say it, Mitch, but if it weren't for you helping me, being there, I would have put a gun to my head by now."

Mitch's heart ached for his friend's pain. "You'll get through this Danny," he said. "You can count on me, I'll help in any way I can."

"You're a good man," Dan said. "I'm glad you were there for Cyn."

They sat in silence.

Dan's gaze returned to the window. He wiped his eyes.

"Remember how I laughed when you said you were thinking about pathology?"

"I remember." Mitch nodded. "Your choice for me was gynecology."

"Best doctoring job I can think of," Dan said. "Lots of perks." He turned to Mitch. "Look at you, you handsome bastard, the women would be lining up, you'd get laid for life!"

"That's not how you make that decision, Danny," Mitch said.

"I know." Dan's mouth turned up in a little smile. "But in those days, that was all either of us thought about."

Mitch nodded. "We were young."

" 'Dumb and full of cum,' " Dan said. "It was probably the best time of our lives."

"For you," Mitch said. "You married Cyn."

"And you married Carole Ann."

Mitch leaned back in his chair. "Don't remind me."

"I always thought Carole Ann was a classy woman, Mitch. She had a lot of style, even then. She was sophisticated, not like . . ."

He stopped talking and again looked out the window.

"Not like Cyn?" Mitch said. "Danny, that's what I loved most about her. She had a total lack of pretension. She was free, and completely unpredictable." Mitch warmed to his memory. "She had that great laugh. The damn thing was contagious, you couldn't help but laugh with her, and she didn't give a damn what anyone thought of her. She was a true gift."

Dan looked at him. "I know you had a little crush on her."

"Crush?" Mitch said. "Danny, if you hadn't seen her first, I'd probably be married to her right now."

"It would have been worth it. At least she wouldn't be gone, and you wouldn't be fooling around with that cop," Dan said.

Mitch's face grew serious. "I'm not fooling around, Danny. I'm in love. Star's an amazing woman."

Dan Rayner stared at Mitch, a mean little glint in his alcohol glazed eyes. "Guess it's true."

"What?"

"Once you go black . . ."

Mitch's eyes hardened. "Danny, you're my friend, and I know you're drunk and grieving, so you're not thinking too clearly, but if you say one more word to insult Star, this friendship is over."

Dan hung his head.

"You're right. I'm sorry," he said. "I'm just crazy right now. She seems to be a nice person."

"An incredible person," Mitch said. "And the woman I love."

Dan nodded. "Okay, okay." He stood up, looking out the window. "It's just that I know that black judge got locked up about Cyn's murder, and they let him go." He faced Mitch. "I'm not prejudiced, you know that, but sometimes I think *all* of them should be locked up."

Mitch didn't say anything. He sighed deeply, and folded his hands on his desk.

"Danny."

Rayner's face reddened.

"I'm doing my best here not to let what you're saying get to me," Mitch said. "I know grief makes people say and do things they wouldn't ordinarily. But Judge Robinson was not guilty of anything other than having been seen running in the area on the day Cyn was found. He's your neighbor, he lives off Hamilton's Woods, just as you do. It makes sense that he'd do his running there."

"What about the evidence they found? They wouldn't have just arrested him, with no evidence."

"It was all circumstantial," Mitch said. "There's no case to hang on him."

"Did your girlfriend tell you that?"

"Danny . . ."

Rayner sat back down and leaned forward. "C'mon Mitch, 'fess up. How much does she tell you when you're pillow talking? She's working this case, right? She knows what's happening. Is she hiding stuff . . . are you? Did she pull some strings to get *'the brother'* off?"

Mitch stood up.

Dan Rayner kept talking. "According to the news, she arrested him, then she let him go. Don't tell me it couldn't have been a trick, a scam. You know how dishonest they are, you know the things they do!"

"Danny, you're leaving."

Rayner's face grew redder, an ugly, nasty look settled on him.

"No, I'm not! Don't try to put anything over on me, Mitch. I *know* you, I know your weakness. You never could think straight when pussy was involved. She's probably fucking you and Robinson, too. Goddammit man, we're practically brothers, don't sell me down the river because some black bitch is spreading her legs for you!"

Mitch was around the desk so fast, Dan didn't have time to blink.

The doctor hauled him out of the chair by the lapels of his hand-tailored, black pinstriped Saville Row suit.

Rayner covered his face with his hands. "Don't. Don't hit me, Mitch. Please, don't hit me!"

Mitch stopped himself, his body vibrating with rage. He released Dan Rayner's lapels as if he'd suddenly found himself holding something loathsome.

He stepped back. "Get help, Danny."

Rayner cowered, his head down, unable to look at Mitch.

Without another word, the doctor opened his office door, reached back, grabbed Rayner, and flung him through it.

Dan Rayner lost his footing and fell against the reception desk.

Mitch's secretary looked up. She'd never seen him so angry. His eyes were like green ice.

"Lorraine."

"Yes, Doctor Grant?"

"Have security notify Mr. Rayner's driver that he's on his way out of the building, and send an escort to make sure he doesn't get lost."

Ernestine Henderson sat with Star in a small holding area off the courtroom.

"Thank you for doing what you did, Lieutenant."

"I'm worried about you, Ernestine," Star said. "I just want you to be alright."

Ernestine took Star's hand. "I know, and I'm gonna be fine. The judge said no more than ten years and with good behavior, I can be out in five. I'm getting counseling. It's better than I would have got if I stayed with Willis."

She squeezed Star's hand. "Don't worry, it'll be fine. I got a roof, and I'm gonna go to school in there, and I won't have to worry about nobody beating on me."

"I'll come and see you."

"I know you will," Ernestine said. "Ms. Carson, my lawyer, said I can learn computers in there. I can write you sometime, on that mail thing."

"E-mail," Star said.

"Uh-huh. Will you answer?"

"Absolutely."

They sat quietly for a moment, hand in hand.

Through the glass door, Star could see the bailiff writing something on a stack of papers attached to a battered, gray metal clipboard. Two armed, gray-uniformed guards from the county jail stood near the desk, waiting.

"Looks like they're here for you." She stood. "I guess I should be going."

Ernestine squeezed her hand. "Can I ask you one more thing?"

"Sure."

"Could you tell Judge Robinson how sorry I am about what happened to him?"

Star sat back down. "You know Judge Robinson?"

"Oh, yes," Ernestine said. "Him and Willis grew up together. They liked to call themselves 'the Jamison Boys' you know, 'cause they grew up in the Jamison Projects.

"When we was first married, Harlan and Joyce was our closest friends. That was when he was still a lawyer, before he got famous and everything." She looked down at her hands. "I been shamed to contact him, with him and Willis being so close, you know, with what I did and all."

Star nodded, dumbfounded.

"But I don't want him to think that I don't care about him. I know he didn't kill that woman, Harlan couldn't even step on a bug. Joyce had to kill the spiders in their house."

CHAPTER FOURTEEN

Star tossed her coat on the chair at her desk and headed toward Captain Lewis's office.

"Hey!" Paresi said. "Who set fire to you?"

She turned. "I've got to talk to the captain."

"He's not in there," Paresi said. "What's going on?"

She walked back to her desk. "Where is he?"

Paresi shrugged. "I don't know. I haven't seen him since this morning." He indicated her chair. "Sit. I got news."

"So have I."

"Me, first," Paresi said.

She sat down. "Okay."

He slid a plastic bag across the desk to her.

"Take a look at that."

Star picked it up.

"What is this?"

"A rear heel light from a pair of top of the line Trailblazers."

"Where did you get it?"

"Some guy walking his dog this morning in Hamilton's Woods found it. He'd been reading in the paper about the case, and they mentioned the shoes with the lights. He found this a few yards from where the body was found."

Star just sat, staring at him.

"So, this is a break; why don't you look happy?" She leaned toward him.

"We need a warrant for Willis Henderson's house and locker, and we need it now."

Star and Paresi opened the door to Willis Henderson's house.

"The last time I was here, I nearly got beaned by a plaster Baby Jesus."

"What?" Paresi said.

"I'll tell you later."

The house had a cold, dark, unpleasant smell. Star took a deep breath. "Already, I'm not liking this."

They stood in the nearly empty living room. Star flipped the light switch. Nothing happened.

"Ernestine's sister is cleaning out the place," she said. "I guess she's already had the electricity shut off."

"Where do we start?"

"The bedroom. We should hit it while we still have some daylight left."

They went to the rear of the house. One lone pink, fuzzy slipper lay in the doorway of the master suite. The bed, stripped of linens and pillows, displayed a king-sized, uncomfortable-looking blue mattress. The windows, stripped of curtains and blinds, added to the eeriness of the room.

"I hate doing this," Star muttered.

"Not me." Paresi slipped on a pair of latex gloves and went to the closet. "I love it." He opened the door and looked inside. He slid clothing along the rack. "Nothing in here but men's clothes. I guess the sisters share the same opinion of Willis."

They began moving items onto the bed. Paresi pulled out a large, heavy, cardboard box.

"Let's start here." He set the box on the mattress, and opened it.

"Just junk," he said, pulling out the contents.

"Look at this." Star pulled a pair of latex gloves from her pants pocket and put them on. She picked up an old high school yearbook. "Dunbar High . . ." She opened it. "Ernestine said Willis and Judge Robinson have been friends since they were kids." She turned the pages, reading the names of the young, hopeful faces.

"Here." She pointed to a handsome, smiling Willis Henderson. "Willis Xavier Henderson, Band, English Club, ROTC, Basketball Team," she read. "He was cute."

"Would you have dated him?"

"He wouldn't have asked me out," Star said. "I was five foot eight at thirteen. Believe me, he *wouldn't* have asked me out."

"Why not? He was on the basketball team," Paresi said.

"Precisely." Star turned the pages. "Basketball players only dated four-foot-eleven-inch cheerleaders. Guys who were shorter than your attention span, *they* loved me."

Paresi laughed.

"Look, here he is." She angled the book into the fading daylight. "Harlan Dubois Robinson, Band, ROTC, English Club, Debate Team, and Captain, Track Team. Looks like he and Willis shared a lot of extracurricular stuff."

" 'Cept, Judge Robinson was on the track team," Paresi said.

"He was the captain."

"So Ernestine said they grew up together and stayed close?"

"Yeah," Star said. "And judging from this, they shared a lot of the same interests, too. I know Willis played piano and drums. He used to play with some jazz band every now and then in a club down on Claremont Street." She looked again at the picture of a teenaged Harlan Robinson. "I wonder what the judge plays? With those beautiful lips, I'll bet he plays a wind instrument."

"Beautiful lips?" Paresi said, grinning.

"Yeah." She pointed. "He was fine then, and he's still good-looking."

Paresi shook his head.

She closed the book and put it on top of the bed. "What?"

"Nothing."

"You're a pig, Paresi." She ignored his laugh and went back to the closet.

"I wonder why Willis never said anything about knowing Judge Robinson. He liked to brag about everything else."

Paresi shrugged, and continued looking through the box.

"Dunno. Maybe he thought hanging with a judge could be like a conflict of interest if it got out. You know, like if he had a perp that went in front of his friend."

She didn't answer.

"Star?" He turned. She was on her knees, tugging something from the back of the closet.

He went to her. "What are you doing?"

"There's something back here." Her voice was muffled by the clothes hanging around her upper body. "It's heavy, give me a hand."

Paresi got down on his knees. "Move."

She moved over, and backed out from the closet. He tugged the heavy box out into the fading light. "Damn . . . what's he got in here?"

"It's not that," Star said, delving back into the darkness, "it's this." She pulled an item from the space near where the box had been, and again backed out on her knees.

She looked at Paresi.

His azure eyes locked with hers. "Trailblazer. Top of the line?"

Star turned the shoe over. The three indented arrows were caked with dried, smeared mud. A very faint, brownish-looking stain clung to the toe of the shoe. Star pulled the leather tongue back and looked inside.

"Size twelve," she said.

"Is the other one in there?"

"I didn't see it."

"Let's keep looking."

The two of them crawled deep into the closet, pulling boxes and cartons away from the back wall.

"Nothing."

They sat on the floor.

Star looked again at the dirty shoe. She lightly touched the soiled toe with her gloved fingertip. "Do you think this is blood?"

Paresi shrugged. "It's been cleaned. It could be dirt or even dog shit . . . can't tell without a test."

Star raised her head and sniffed the air.

"Paresi." She sniffed again.

"What?"

"What do you smell?"

Paresi sniffed the air. "Closet funk, and that filthy shoe."

"There's something else." Star sniffed again. "It's faint, but it smells like the autopsy room . . . death, and some kind of cleaner, like . . ." She sniffed again. "Like Pine Sol."

Paresi lifted an eyebrow. "When the full moon rises, do you howl?"

"Only if you're out," she said, getting to her feet. "Help me."

Paresi stood and together they began tearing and tossing the hanging clothing from the closet to the bed. Finally the space was bare, except for the boxes they'd moved from the wall.

Paresi reached into his pocket and pulled out a small, blue Magnalite flashlight.

"Over here." He beamed the light, exposing a loose board near the bottom of the closet.

"Here." He handed her the light. "Stand back."

Star moved a few inches away, and watched Paresi wrestle the plank of wood from the wall. As he pulled it free, the matching Trailblazer shoe fell at his feet.

Star picked it up and shined the light on it.

"Now this *is* blood." She turned it around. "Lots of it, and no safety light." She turned it again. "There's mud here, too, smeared. Maybe he didn't have time to clean it off."

Paresi shook his head as if to clear it.

"Gimme some light." He crouched by the ripped board. "There's something else in here."

Star aimed the light over his shoulder, directly onto the torn panel. Paresi grabbed the loose wood with both hands and pulled it completely away from the wall. A dull silver gleam shone in the cave-like opening of the rear of the closet.

Star aimed the light at the object. Paresi reached in, pulling it from the back wall.

"Light me," he said.

Star angled the illumination at the long, dully glistening item in her partner's gloved hand.

It was an aluminium baseball bat. Star moved the light down the length of it, exposing dried, smeared reddish brown stains, chunks of clinging, decayed flesh, bits of brain tissue, and long curly strands of champagne blonde hair.

"Batter up," Paresi said.

"Down there." Star again pointed at the hole in the wall. An institutional-sized bottle of Pine Sol cleaner lay open and upended. The cap was missing, and its contents had spilled out, soaked, and then dried into a solid oil-like mass onto the splintered wood. The now faint but unmistakable smell of Pine Sol wafted from the hole.

Paresi looked at Star. "I'd say he was in a major hurry when he threw this stuff in here."

Star nodded. "Yeah, he was cleaning up and some-body was coming, so he just tossed it all into the hole. The bottle wasn't capped right, so it spilled."

Paresi shook his head and raised the bat. "This thing had to stink to high heaven, and with all that cleaner spilled back here, wouldn't you think his wife would have smelled it . . . said something?"

"Ernestine was afraid of him," Star said. "I'm sure she just opened the window. It was a lot safer than trying to search around inside this closet."

Paresi looked at Star. In the faded light she saw the look in his eyes. "This guy was a cop. He was one of us."

"I know," she said softly. "It hurts."

CHAPTER FIFTEEN

Robin Grant had the doorman leave her Louis Vuitton bags in the foyer of her father's penthouse apartment. She tipped him twenty dollars.

When she closed the door, she tossed her bright blue Missoni cashmere jacket and gray Vuitton handbag on the bench opposite the armoire and went into the kitchen. She opened Mitch's subzero refrigerator and searched the shelves.

"Bingo." She reached inside. "I know my dad."

The bottle of Cristàl champagne was perfectly chilled. She popped the cork and put her mouth over the top of the foaming bottle.

"Mmmmmm." She sighed, and then took a long drink of the effervescent wine.

"What else is in here?" She leaned down, looking at the contents of the refrigerator. She lifted the cover from a plastic storage container.

"Chicken. Excellent."

She grabbed a wing and twisted, ripping off a considerable amount of the breast as well. She dipped her fingers in the sauce beneath the portion she'd just torn off, and licked them.

"Mmmm—outstanding."

Sucking her fingers, Robin used her hip to bump the refrigerator door closed. She neglected to return the cover to the container.

With the chicken and the bottle of champagne, she walked into the living room, plopped down on Mitch's leather sofa, kicked off her pewter gray Vuitton loafers, put her feet up on the coffee table, and started to eat.

"God, I love Jerk Chicken," she said out loud. "And Dad, this is the best I've had since Mom took me to Jamaica." Again, she drank from the champagne bottle, ate more chicken, then licked her fingers and looked around at the apartment.

"Lots of changes since the last time I was here." Her gaze wandered up the stairs. "Let's see what you're up to these days."

She took the last bite of the chicken, dropped the nearly clean wing bone on the coffee table, and got up. Still carrying the champagne, she climbed the stairs, leaving a greasy trail of Jerk sauce on the polished, oak bannister.

She stopped at the loft, which held Mitch's library. A book lay open on the table next to one of his Eames chairs.

"Let's see what you're reading." She peered at the book, only to be met by a color photo of a naked dead man with staring eyes. His entire body cavity had been opened, displaying his internal organs.

"Oh, gross!" Robin turned away. "Jesus Dad, nobody likes looking at that shit but you. Ugh!" She covered her mouth and breathed deeply until her stomach settled again.

She went back to the stairs and on to the top floor.

Mitch's bedroom door was open. Robin stood, looking inside.

"Now *this* is a bedroom," she said, walking in slowly. She stood in front of her father's huge, specially made bed. "What a party I could have on that thing."

She walked over to the floor-to-ceiling windows.

"Excellent view," she said, taking a swig of champagne.

She caught sight of a stack of CDs sitting atop a table near the fireplace. She set the bottle down on the hardwood floor, and went through them with her still greasy fingers.

"James Taylor, Elton John, what are they, a hundred? The sixties are *so* over, Dad, it's the Year One again, get a clue."

She shuffled through some more. "Chris Isaak. Hmmmm, there might be some hope for you. . . . The Spinners? Keb' Mo', Z. Z. Hill, '*Down Home Blues,*' what is this stuff?" She slid the plastic cases over and under each other. "Jimmy Reed, *Mary Wells' Greatest Hits*? Who's Mary Wells? The

Temptations, *tragic!*" She tossed the CDs back atop the table.

Picking up the bottle of champagne, she went into Mitch's dressing room and turned on the lights.

Her father's clothes had always intrigued her. As old guys go, he was good-looking.

From the time she could remember, all of her girlfriends—not to mention their mothers—from kindergarten to Brown University, had swooned when her dad was on the scene. Even that horrible woman, Emma Erickson, who taught literature and made them read Doris Lessing's *The Golden Notebook*, when she was a senior in high school.

Robin had sworn the teacher was a lesbian until she saw the facial-hair-challenged Ms. Erickson practically have an orgasm when her father shook her hand in the school parking lot.

He was wearing a jet-black, pinstriped, double-breasted Armani suit that day, and gold-rimmed, Gucci sunglasses. Robin thought he looked like a mafia boss. All he needed was dark hair. He had come to pick her up on a Friday, to begin one of their rare weekends together.

She walked from cabinet to cabinet, like a visitor in a museum, viewing her father's clothes. There were suits, sweaters, shoes, all displayed in easy access, built-in alcoves. There were even shelves for jeans, and multicolored folded stacks of sweatshirts and tees.

"No muscle tees, huh Dad?" she said, viewing

the neat stacks. Her father had a great body for a guy his age. She stopped, a little smile on her lips. Hell, for a guy any age, even though she'd rather die than admit it. He was long and lean, and he wore everything from hand-tailored Italian suits, to jeans, with style. Now that she was older, she could see why women loved him so much.

"And he's wasting it all on one," she muttered.

In the center of the large room sat an island cabinet with glass drawers. Robin could see shirts, ties folded neatly, socks, and underwear. As she turned, another built-in table held various men's colognes, and a red lacquered Chinese box. She remembered it from her childhood. It held her father's collection of tie tacks, tiepins, and cuff links. Next to that was a smaller cabinet holding six tailored tuxedos.

Floor-to-ceiling mirrors stood in two corners of the room.

Robin turned, about to shut off the lights, when she saw another cabinet, partially filled with women's clothing. Taking another drink from the champagne bottle, she went to it.

She folded her arms and stood back, dangling the half-empty bottle loosely from her fingers. She looked at the array of skirts, pants, dresses, and tops. With her free hand, she reached for a deep purple silk blouse.

"Gross," she muttered, putting it back.

Turning, she left the dressing room and walked into the master bath.

She saw two Sonicare toothbrushes, and alongside her father's toiletries and shaving things, a small, yellow and brown jar, with Afrocentric-styled drawings on the label. She put down the champagne and picked it up.

"Cocoa butter? What the hell is cocoa butter?" She put it back and opened one of the mirrored glass-enclosed medicine cabinets over the double sinks.

"Tampax . . ." She picked up the box of tampons. "Multi-pack, great." She tossed the box back inside, closed the chest, and went back to the dressing room.

There on the table with the red Chinese box was something she'd missed before. Another smaller, lacquered box. This one was black, with pale jade leaves and vines painted on it.

She opened it.

The box contained several makeup brushes, two different shades of eye shadow, a small pot of blush, two black mascara wands, and a compact of MAC makeup. She opened it. The deep bronze color of the makeup made her bite down on her bottom lip.

"I guess mom was right. She *is* living here." Robin closed the compact and put it back. "But not for long."

Her eyes fell on two black tubes of MAC lipstick. She opened the first one, swiveling it from the bottom. A deep ruby red wand of color appeared. She put it back and opened the second one. It revealed a hue somewhere between brown and russet. She put that one back as well.

Closing the black lacquered box, she looked again at the cologne bottles on the table.

Mixed in among her father's scents were several bottles of women's fragrance. She picked them up one by one. Shalimar, Obsession, Oscar de la Renta, Issey Miyake, and 273.

"At least she smells good," Robin said, straightening the bottles.

She turned around slowly to see if she'd missed anything else.

A bathrobe.

It was hanging on the back of the door, closest to the table and the walkway into the bathroom. The robe was deep blue chenille and definitely not her father's. She took it from the burnished gold hook, turning it, looking at it. It was long, and emblazoned with white stars and yellow crescent moons. One pocket held something. She reached in, pulling out a handful of silver-wrapped Hershey's Kisses.

"Gross," she said, putting them back and hanging up the robe. "I'll bet he thinks it's sexy."

Robin went back to the bath, grabbed the bottle of champagne, and left through the bedroom, leaving all the lights on.

She bounded back down the stairs, and plopped

herself on the sofa, waiting for her father to come home.

Mitch and Star got out of the elevator, giggling like teenagers, and kissed their way to his front door, where they only stopped long enough for him to reach into his overcoat pocket.

"Where's my key?"

She laid her head against his chest. "Don't tell me you've lost it."

That made them giggle louder.

"No, I've got it." He fished in his pocket. "Do you have yours?"

They laughed loudly.

Star put her finger to her lips. "Sshhh . . . Let me look." She reached into his pocket.

The two of them had met after work and had dinner at a newly opened excellent Thai restaurant, in the renovated section of Old Brookport.

As they drove to the bistro, they passed Gilstrom's. Star looked out of the opposite window. She'd had a bad enough day. She didn't even want to think about Willis Henderson, Judge Robinson, or the evidence that she and Paresi had turned over before they left for the night.

Mitch told her over dinner about his experience with his drunken and bitter old friend. They agreed that they'd both had enough, and tonight was just for them.

He leaned close, kissing her again.

"I thought you were looking for your keys," she said. "No more Balinese wine for you."

"I'm not drunk," he said.

"No, you just love to see me drive your Porsche."

Mitch pulled her into his arms. "That's because you look so sexy behind the wheel."

He kissed her again. "And when we get inside . . ." He reached into his pocket, taking her hand. "*If* we get inside, I'm going to show you just how drunk I'm not . . . all . . . night . . . long."

"Oh, bay-bay!" she said in a deep Barry White–like voice, as she pulled out his keys. "Let's get this door open."

Giggling and bumping into one another, they entered the darkened penthouse.

Mitch closed the door, leaned his back against it, and pulled Star to him in the shadowy foyer. The kiss was so intense, her knees actually buckled. She clung to him, feeling the heat of his body, savoring the taste of him, the wine, and the evening.

The sudden light was blinding.

They broke apart, like two guilty adolescents.

"Hi, Dad." Robin stood barefoot in the doorway of the living room. "Surprise!"

"Robin?" Mitch took a second to focus.

"Yeah, Dad, are you drunk?"

"No," both Mitch and Star said together.

He took her hand and walked her into the living room.

"Hi, baby." He hugged his daughter. She looked at Star, her mother's blue eyes blank in her pale face.

"So, Dad, is this your latest?"

Mitch stepped away from his daughter.

"Apologize." He put his arm around Star, and pulled her to his side.

Robin folded her arms, her long blonde hair trailed across her cheek. She tossed her head, flipping the hair back.

"I said, *apologize*." Her father's voice let her know he meant it.

Robin sighed. "I'm sorry."

"Like you mean it."

She looked at Star. "I'm sorry, I was very rude."

"Yes, you were," Star said, extending her hand.

"This is Starletta Duvall, Robin," Mitch said. "She's not my latest . . . she's my only."

CHAPTER SIXTEEN

"You look as bad as I feel," Paresi said, as Star hung up her coat and flung her purse loudly into her bottom desk drawer.

"What a charmer," she said, sitting down.

"Rough night?"

"Let's just say that being in a stinking closet with a bloody, crud-encrusted baseball bat was about the high point of my day."

Paresi laughed. "Join the club."

"You, too?" she said.

"I had a fight with Vee last night."

"About?"

"My being an idiot." He looked at her. "I'm sure she'll tell you the story, then I'll give you my side."

"If your side involves yesterday's happenings, I understand," Star said.

"Tell *her*," Paresi said.

"Don't worry, Vee hates the job, but she understands it. She never stays mad. Anger is not a permanent thing with her, unlike little Miss Robin Grant."

Paresi raised an eyebrow. "His kid's here?"

"Yep. She showed up last night to surprise him."

"And you?" Paresi said.

"Yeah, well, I was a little taken aback."

"What's she like?"

"Bitch-in-training," Star said. "But I don't want to talk about it." She nodded toward the door. "I saw a bunch of boxes down in the lobby when I came in . . . think they might be headed this way?"

"Yeah." Paresi pulled the top file from the mound in the tray on his desk. "Overnight went to Willis's house and took all the boxes from the garage and his car. They also found three containers of Neptune's Haven pool cleaner in his garage. Two liquid, one crystals, and all of them nearly empty. As soon as everything gets checked in, we're going to have more searching to do."

"Oh, goody," Star said. "I need chocolate." She stood up yawning, and stretched. "I'm going upstairs, you want something?"

"Yeah, why don't you lay a big wet one on Elvis, and get him to part with one of those humongous apple muffins."

Star put her hands on her hips. "Whatever Vee's ticked about with you, I'm on her side."

The boxes from Willis Henderson's property took up all of the long table in the rear of the squad room. Three large bottles of Neptune's Haven pool cleaner, also found in his garage, sat tagged underneath.

More boxes were stacked hip high next to Star and Paresi's desks. They sat with Chuck Richardson, surrounded by empty coffee mugs, water bottles, and the remains of Paresi's apple muffin, while they painstakingly picked through the contents. Star's phone rang.

"Homicide, Lieutenant Duvall."

"Good morning." Mitch's voice was soft in her ear. She turned her chair away from Chuck and Paresi. "Good morning. How are you?"

"Lonely," he said. "I missed you last night. I don't sleep well without you in my arms."

Star blushed. "Me, too, but I thought it best if I went home."

"You're probably right." He sighed. "Robin and I had a talk this morning, even though she had a hell of a hangover."

"Hangover?"

"She drank the bottle of Cristàl I had chilling for us."

"The whole bottle?"

"It was definitely too much of a good thing."

"Isn't she too young to drink?" Star said.

Mitch laughed. "Yes, she's nineteen, going on forty-five."

Star nodded. " 'Nuff said. How is she?"

"Do you care?" She could hear his smile. "Or are you being polite?"

"Uh . . . the second one."

He laughed.

She smiled.

"I don't blame you. She was rude, but she now understands how important you are in my life. In fact, she wants to make it up. She wants us to have dinner together. Are you willing?"

"Let's talk about it later," she said. "Did you call just to say hi?"

"No," Mitch said. "I've got the autopsy report on Willis Henderson. Whenever you and Paresi can get over here, we've got some things to discuss."

She turned her chair back. "Okay, this afternoon."

"See you then," Mitch said. "I love you."

She smiled. "Me too, you."

When she hung up, both Paresi and Chuck were sitting there, hands folded under their chins, grinning and fluttering their eyelashes.

"Grow up you guys!" she said, laughing in spite of herself.

"So what's he got besides the obvious?" Paresi said.

"The information on Willis Henderson's autopsy. He wants us in his office as soon as we can get there."

"Why don't you guys go ahead," Chuck said. "I can go through the rest of this stuff by myself."

"Sure?" Star asked.

"Yeah." Chuck nodded.

Star looked at Paresi. "Well, we could go see Mitchell, and then head over to Judge Robinson's court afterward."

"Okay," Paresi said.

Star turned to Chuck. "You sure you don't mind?"

"No, go on. I'll do this. See you guys later."

She looked at Paresi. "Let's go."

Joyce Robinson stood in the doorway of her husband's bedroom. She hadn't spoken to him since he'd been arrested. Everything their lives had been based on was crumbling beneath their feet.

Because of her problem and her love for Harlan, she'd allowed him to have a life separate from theirs together. All she'd asked was that he be discreet, and always come home to her.

For years, that had worked. But now . . . She'd never counted on the humiliation, the shame of his being locked up, suspected of killing a white woman. She wrung her hands. A white woman.

He'd never mentioned Cynthia Chapin-Rayner, but Joyce always felt there was something in the air between them. She remembered the very first day Harlan met the woman. She could still see the way Cynthia Rayner's eyes traveled over her husband's body.

She shuddered.

The wood of the doorway against her arms felt cold.

"How could he do this?" She wrapped her arms around herself, holding tightly, while still feeling as if her life were somehow leaking right out through her pores. "How could he do this to me!"

She couldn't breathe. Her eyes watered.

She looked out of his window.

The morning sun had shifted.

How long had she been standing in the doorway? How long had she been blind to what her husband was doing with that white woman?

In all of their years of marriage, she had never deliberately violated his privacy before, but now, she had to know.

"Willis Henderson's body had several cuts and old scars," Mitch said, laying the autopsy photos on the table in the conference room. "You can see he had fresh scrapes and bruises on his right leg."

"He'd been in a SWAT situation shortly before Cynthia Rayner's murder," Star said. "If you didn't suspect anything, you'd just think the injuries occurred there."

"I agree," Mitch said. "That's why I haven't said anything to Dr. Rao."

"Dr. Rao?" Paresi asked.

Mitch pointed to the copy of the report in Paresi's hand. "When you get the chance to look at that, you'll see I didn't perform the autopsy. Willis was brought in on the same morning that Cyn was discovered. I worked on her."

He arranged more photos on the table. "Dr. Rao did a very thorough job. He's new to our team, and he's an excellent pathologist. To him, Willis was a routine procedure."

"Nobody thought anything else," Star said.

"Exactly," Mitch agreed. "So, this now makes a lot of sense." He handed the detectives a photo of Willis Henderson's right hand.

"See it?" Mitch said.

"A bite." Star traced the wound with her finger. "It's a good one, too."

"Willis's blood matched the blood on Cyn's panties," Mitch said. "AB, with a dormant sickle-cell trait."

"Why didn't Doctor Rao report this?" Paresi said.

"He did." Mitch put his hands in the pockets of his blue scrubs. "It's in the report. The fault is mine. I've been so wrapped up with Danny, and this whole thing, that I missed it. I didn't read the report as thoroughly as I should have. I was just too preoccupied trying to help a guy I thought was my friend."

"Thought?" Paresi said.

"It's a long story." Mitch walked around the table. "Bottom line, this is my mistake, and I take full responsibility."

"Don't beat yourself up," Paresi said. "Willis wasn't even in anybody's mind as being connected with this."

"He's right," Star said, sitting down. "None of us knew anything about his life outside the station, other than his beating his wife; and it took her shooting him to remind us of that." She indicated Paresi. "We still have to talk to Judge Robinson about his friendship with Willis. Obviously, Willis killed Cynthia Rayner. The question is why," Star said. "And just how much does Judge Robinson know?"

CHAPTER SEVENTEEN

Harlan saw Star and her partner enter the courtroom and take a seat in the rear. He had expected it. As soon as the witness on the stand was finished, he called a recess.

As the courtroom cleared, he stood and pointed toward his chambers. Star and Paresi waited for the room to empty and followed him inside.

"Judge Robinson, I'm sorry about the incidents leading up to our having to arrest you," Star said.

Harlan Robinson kept his eyes down. He sat heavily in the black leather chair behind his desk. The detectives settled in the two chairs in front of it.

"It was humiliating, but I understand. You were doing your job." He looked at her briefly. "As your father always did his."

Star didn't like his tone, but she let it go.

"Be that as it may, we had evidence . . ."

"Circumstantial," the judge interrupted.

"Circumstantial," Star said, "but evidence just the same."

"Strong enough to haul you in," Paresi said coldly.

"But not strong enough to keep me." Harlan stared eye-to-eye at the detective.

Paresi smiled. *"Yet."*

The judge turned back to Star, meeting her eyes briefly. "Get to the point, Lieutenant."

"The point, Your Honor, is that we know who killed Cynthia Chapin-Rayner."

Harlan blanched beneath his dark skin. "Who?" he managed to say.

"A police officer," Star said, watching him intently. "A SWAT officer named Willis Henderson. Do you know him?"

Harlan's hands shook. He put them into his lap, out of view under the desk. "No."

"That's strange." Star leaned forward. "You were at his funeral. I saw you."

"Henderson, did you say?"

"I did." Star's gaze intensified.

"Yes, I did make an appearance at his funeral. I'm a black judge, Lieutenant, and Mr. . . . Henderson, is it?"

Star nodded.

"Mr. Henderson was a member of the police department and the black community. It's only right that I should have been there."

Star regarded him intently, letting his words hang in the tense atmosphere before she spoke. "Mr. Henderson was also your lifelong friend."

Robinson shook his head. "No . . . no. . . ."

"Don't do that, Judge Robinson," she said.

"Do what?"

"Lie." Her gaze caught and held him. He saw his old nemesis, Len Duvall, regarding him from behind his daughter's eyes.

"We know about your relationship with Willis Henderson. His wife told us."

"Ernestine killed him!" Harlan exploded. "She's a murderer! Why would you believe anything she'd have to say to you?"

"You know her name," Star said.

Robinson blinked, his eyes darted around the room. "It was in the paper. I read it, or I heard it on the news."

"I see." Star reached into the oversized satchel purse she was carrying and laid Willis Henderson's high school yearbook on the judge's desk.

"Did you hear about this on the news, too?"

Harlan regarded the yearbook as if Star had deposited a poisonous snake on top of his desk.

She sat back in the chair. "You want to tell us about 'the Jamison Boys'?"

Joyce had gone through the closets and all of the drawers in Harlan's dresser and highboy. A thin sheen of sweat covered her face, and her stomach kept twisting around itself. She sat on the edge of his king-sized bed and wiped her face with a Kleenex from the box on his bedside table.

"There's nothing here," she muttered, shredding the tissue in her hands. "Not a damned thing."

She stood, and her eye caught the antique map on the wall, opposite his bed.

"The chest!" Her face lit up. "That chest in his study."

She tossed the tissue into the wastebasket and practically ran through the house.

The sun, having moved around the house, seemed to point directly at it. Mote-filled beams shone down on the weather-beaten sea chest on the floor against the wall, next to Harlan's mahogany glass-doored law book cases.

They had bought the aged sea chest on a weekend trip to Gloucester during the first year of their marriage. They'd found it in an old, cluttered antique shop, the kind they used to spend hours poking around in. She pulled it away from the wall and lifted the lid.

There, beneath the old news clippings and law journals, she found it.

A black plastic videotape box.

She pulled it out and opened it.

"Do I want to see this?" she asked herself out loud.

Her body, not waiting for an answer, was already moving toward the TV and VCR in the cabinet on the opposite wall. With trembling hands, Joyce turned on the VCR and slipped the tape into the machine.

She went back to Harlan's desk, and picked up the remote.

Before turning on the TV, she closed her eyes, praying not to see what she already knew was on that tape.

With tears in her eyes, and her palms slick with sweat, she pushed the button that started the tape.

"Oh my God." She put her hand to her mouth. "Oh my God."

The tape playing on the screen showed a happy, smiling Joyce and a loving, attentive Harlan.

"It's our anniversary," she whispered. "Our fifteenth. Oh, thank you, God."

She relaxed, watching the images of the two of them, surrounded by friends, toasting one another, laughing.

"What a wonderful party this was." She put the remote down, letting herself get lost in the memory playing before her.

She looked so happy . . . she *was* so happy. Joyce clasped her hands together.

Suddenly the merry visages were replaced by a blank blue screen.

"What happened?" Joyce picked up the remote, and pushed the button, fast forwarding the tape.

The figures racing across the screen had nothing to do with her anniversary.

Joyce rewound the tape and pushed the play button.

Her legs wouldn't hold her; she dropped to her knees.

The remote fell from her hand and bounced on the thickness of the plush, pale gray carpet.

Joyce's stomach lurched. She thought she would be sick, but she was too shocked to even vomit.

Her heart stopped, hanging in her chest like some horrific frozen thing.

She was numb, oblivious to the fact that her fingernails were gouging deep crevices into the flesh of her arms.

On the screen, her husband was bringing Cynthia Chapin-Rayner to a writhing, back-scratching, screaming orgasm.

Harlan Dubois Robinson sat staring at the two detectives.

"We can talk here, or down at the station," Star said, reaching for the yearbook.

Robinson put his hand on the book. "Here," he said. "Let's talk here."

Star sat back in her chair.

The judge took a deep breath.

"Willis and I knew one another since the first grade. We both grew up in that cesspool over on Fremont Street."

"The Jamison Projects," Star said.

"Yes." Harlan nodded. "We bonded from the beginning. It was as if we knew, even from that early age, what we both wanted, and that was to get out. As we grew, so did our desire."

He finally looked directly at her.

"And it was fierce, Lieutenant. Our whole world was boxed into eight city blocks of high-rise slums filled with poverty-stricken, ignorant, drunken, drug-addled, dangerous people.

"Willis and I used to be called faggots because we chose to study rather than be 'men' and lie down in some filthy hole on a piss-smelling mattress and help some no-class slut qualify for a bigger welfare check.

"We had to fight just to go to school." Harlan's face twisted at the memory. "Sometimes they'd wait for us at the bus stop and kick our asses, simply because we had books in our hands, and not drugs."

"Judge Robinson, I don't see . . ."

"No, you *don't* see," he interrupted her. "You grew up in a nice house, in a nice neighborhood."

She opened her mouth, he pointed a finger at her.

"I *know* you had a good life. Because I knew your father. When I first came on the bench, we clashed almost every time he came before me."

"I'm aware of that," Star said, "but that has no . . ."

Judge Robinson talked over her.

"He was always in my face about being too tough on the 'brothers.' He wanted me to give those ignorant, know-nothing, want-nothing, got-nothing niggers a break when they came before me. I wouldn't. Nobody gave me a break. I hustled, and so did Willis. We *worked* our way out of that hellhole."

"That's all very laudable, Judge Robinson," Star said coldly. "But it doesn't tell me why Willis Henderson would kill Cynthia Chapin-Rayner."

"He wouldn't," Robinson said. "Not deliberately. If he did, it was an accident."

Paresi, who had been barely able to tolerate the judge's words, exploded.

"You pompous bastard!" Paresi was on his feet.

"You sit there and talk about how hard you had it, lumping a whole neighborhood of people into the category of losers and assholes; then you say if your good friend killed this woman, it was an accident."

He shook his head incredulously. "How the fuck can you sit there, with that smug fucking look and say accident? The woman was beaten, asphyxiated, thrown in a pit, and had a caustic chemical poured on her. Nobody's fucking traumatic upbringing is worth that."

Star reached out for him.

"No." Paresi shrugged her hand off his arm.

"Tell me, Judge Robinson, just what was your homeboy Willis doing out in Hamilton's Woods? How could he have such a terrible accident? What? Was he swinging a bat, getting in a little practice, and she put her head in the way?"

Paresi leaned over the man's desk, his blue eyes dark and glacial.

"Okay, let's say I'll buy that, but tell me, what was he trying to do when he *accidentally* shoved her panties down her throat? Or how about when he stumbled and *accidentally* tossed her into a pit?"

Robinson's face was ashen.

"Paresi . . ." Star reached for him again.

"No." He walked a few feet from the desk.

She knew there was no stopping him, and in all honesty, she didn't want to. She agreed with everything he was saying. This man, who was so proud of what he'd accomplished, was doing exactly what the poor and hopeless did when they came before him. He was dumping his sins, and those of his friend, on his environment.

Somewhere in this lesson, Harlan Robinson would come face-to-face with the reality of who and what he was, and she didn't want to miss it.

Star sat back, her eyes on his face. Behind her, her partner was pacing.

"I need to think about this," Paresi said, folding his arms, looking at Robinson. "You gotta be right. It all must have been accidental."

His eyes, like Star's, were on the judge.

"I can see it now. Your good friend Willis must have picked up a bottle of pool cleaner, you know, to get this caustic substance out of the way, so nobody would get hurt, and it what? Leaked out, and just happened to form a trail?"

Paresi threw his hands in the air.

"Hey! That could happen. Then maybe your accident-prone pal was so shocked by the leakage that he tripped and some of the chemical just *happened* to fall on this woman, who he'd *accidentally* flung into a pit." He turned his palms outward.

"This was just not his day, because then matches just *fell* out of his pocket and *accidentally* started a fire, which would have burned her beyond recognition, if it hadn't rained."

He sat down, his eyes still on Harlan. "Yeah, that could happen."

Judge Robinson put his hands over his face.

Paresi leaned forward, his forearms resting on his knees, his blue eyes nearly black. "Tell the truth, Your Honor, and tell it now."

Robinson's shoulders began to shake.

"I loved her," he said softly. "I loved her, but I couldn't do what she wanted."

"Which was?" Star said.

He hung his head. "She wanted to marry me. She was pregnant with my child. She wanted to tell her husband and end her marriage. She asked me to leave Joyce and marry her." A tear slid down his face. "I couldn't. . . ."

"So you had her killed?" Star said.

"No." Robinson wiped his eyes. "No, I didn't."

The detectives sat looking at him.

"Willis knew Cyn and I were lovers. I confided in him," Judge Robinson said. "I told him about the pregnancy. I told him she wanted to divorce her husband, and marry me. I told him everything."

Judge Robinson's shoulders trembled again; a great sob escaped him.

"If she had divorced Dan Rayner, it would have been news, and all of it would have come out."

"Are you saying Willis acted on his own, to protect you?" Star said.

The judge shook his head. "I don't know." He wiped his eyes. "He knew how hard I'd worked . . . how hard we'd *both* worked to get out of Jamison, to have decent lives. He knew if this affair was made public, I'd lose everything—my wife, my standing in the community, my credibility, everything."

"So he removed the problem for you," Star said.

"I don't know," Robinson sobbed. "He wouldn't just kill her without reason. He wouldn't have."

Star and Paresi looked at one another, as the judge wept. Finally, he wiped his face and looked at them.

"I don't know anything about this. I honestly don't." A deep sob escaped him. "All I know is she's gone and my best friend is dead, too."

Star's beeper went off just as she and Paresi got to their car.

"Can I use your phone?"

He reached into his pocket and pulled out his cell phone.

"Why don't you carry yours?"

She shrugged. "Because I hate 'em." She punched

the number onto the keypad. "They cause cancer, you know."

"So does breathing," Paresi said.

She held the phone a little distance from her ear. "You really should get one of those earpiece thingies."

Paresi shook his head and leaned against the car.

"Hi, Chuck," she said into the phone. "What's up?"

Chuck Richardson looked at the paper in his hand. "You guys wrapped up yet?"

"Just about," Star said. "What've you got?"

"Just get back to the house, A.S.A.P.," Chuck said.

"We're on the way."

CHAPTER EIGHTEEN

Chuck Richardson was standing near the squad room double doors when they came in.

"It's about time."

"We got back as soon as we could," Star said. "What's the emergency?"

"Over here," he beckoned.

They followed.

"I was just about to give it up for a while, get something to eat, when I found this." He pointed to a box on Star's desk.

"A Trailblazer shoe box," she said. "We've got the shoes."

Chuck handed her a pair of latex gloves. "Open it."

Star pulled on the gloves and lifted the top off of the red-white-and-blue-striped carton.

"Oh my!"

Paresi whistled.

Chuck grinned.

"Holy shit!" Paresi looked at the other two detectives. "How much do you think is in there?"

"Don't have a clue," Richardson said. "Loman's coming down to pick it up and have it dusted and counted."

Star pointed to the hundred-dollar bills bundled with rubber bands and neatly stacked in the box.

"If they're all hundreds, there's got to be at least a quarter of a million in here. Willis must have been some piano player."

"Yeah, a traveling one." Chuck handed her a plastic-wrapped rectangular slip of paper. "Check out his itinerary."

Star looked at the paper through the plastic bag. "This is an airline ticket."

"Not exactly," Chuck said. "Look again."

She put it on her desk and smoothed the plastic. Paresi looked over her shoulder. "It's a boarding pass."

"Yep," Chuck said.

"It's for DeLiberti," Star said, looking at Paresi.

Her partner nodded. "Private plane."

"And who just told us he flew DeLiberti the day his wife was murdered?" Chuck said.

"Dan Rayner." Star reached for the phone.

Robin Grant sat in her father's outer office, inspecting her nails and trying to ignore the fact that his secretary was staring at her.

"You look a lot like your daddy," Lorraine said.

"I know," Robin said flatly. "Everybody tells me that."

"Well, he's very handsome," the secretary said.

Robin looked at her. "Have you fucked him?"

Lorraine's mouth dropped open.

Mitch walked into the office. "Hi, baby . . ."

The look on his assistant's face made him turn to his daughter. "What did you do?"

Robin sighed extravagantly and rolled her eyes. "Nothing. I'm just waiting for you so that we can get something to eat." She stood up, indicating his blue scrubs. "You are changing, aren't you?"

"No," he said. "I'm wearing these." He indicated a dark spot. "Think anybody will notice this little bit of liver here?"

"Oh, gross, Dad; not funny."

"Sit tight," he said. "Let me clean up." He opened his office door. "You can wait in here, if you want."

Robin got up, glanced at Lorraine, and sauntered into his office.

"I'm sorry, Lorraine."

"Whatever for?" she said, both her smile and her Southern belle drawl working overtime.

"For whatever she said to you. I know she said something, I could tell by the look on your face, not to mention the atmosphere. She's willful and rude, so I apologize."

Lorraine rested her frosted pink-nailed fingers on her ample bosom. "It's okay Mitch, I know all about little girls. I used to be one myself. I know what life is like when you're that young."

The doctor looked relieved. "Thanks."

He went into his office.

Lorraine watched him close the door.

"Little bitch," she muttered, her eyes narrowing. "Yes, I have fucked your daddy, little girl," she said between clenched teeth. "And he loved it."

She slammed a pen down on her desk, her blue eyes blazed.

"And when he gets tired of walking in the jungle, I'm gonna get him back." She looked over her shoulder at Mitch's closed door. "So watch out little Miss Robin, I just might end up being your stepmama."

The phone rang.

"Dr. Grant's office."

"Hi, Lorraine, this is Starletta Duvall. I need to talk to Dr. Grant. It's urgent."

"One moment, Lieutenant." Lorraine put Star on hold.

"Can this day get any better?"

She pushed the intercom button.

Robin answered. "What?"

"This is an urgent call for your father," Lorraine said.

"He's in the shower, take a message." Robin hit the button, cutting her off.

Lorraine took a deep breath, and tapped the

remaining lit button on her phone. "Hold on Lieutenant Duvall, it's gon' be a minute."

She got up and went into Mitch's office.

Ignoring Robin sitting in her father's chair, Lorraine crossed the large room. She opened the door to the private bath, stepped inside, and closed it behind her.

"Mitch," she called out over the rushing water. "Lieutenant Duvall is on the line; she says it's an emergency."

Robin heard the water stop, and then her father's voice.

"Tell her I'll be right there."

Lorraine stepped back into the office and closed the bathroom door. She walked past the glowering Robin. "Does that answer your question, sugah?"

Harlan Robinson arrived home to find his house dark, with no sign of Joyce. He went into the kitchen; it was cold. No dinner, nothing on the stove or in the oven. He checked the bulletin board by the refrigerator; there was no note.

He went into his wife's bedroom. It bore the same coldness. Instinctively, he went to the closet. Her clothes were gone.

He knew, as he approached the den, what he would find.

An eerie, flickering light shone through the open doorway as he entered the otherwise dark room.

The television set, reflecting a white, snowy

screen, glowed in its cabinet. Beneath it, he could see the bright red light of the VCR. It was still on.

Harlan crossed the room to his desk. On top of it, the open, empty black plastic videotape box glowed in the flickering light.

He sat down heavily, his head pounding, a tight feeling in his chest. He looked down at the floor. The remote lay on the carpet, its rounded head pointed at the flickering screen.

He picked it up and pushed the button.

Instantly, the images appeared.

Harlan sat back in his chair, watching himself and Cynthia Chapin-Rayner abandoning themselves to a white-hot passion.

His mind took him back to that night.

It had been her idea to make the tape. She said she wanted him to have something to remind him of their love, when they couldn't be together.

Harlan had been reluctant at first, but he gave in.

Cynthia had brought her video camera and set it up in their hotel room. It was then she realized she'd forgotten to bring a tape. She called him, asking him to bring one. In his haste to get there, he didn't want to stop, so he'd grabbed a tape out of the box Joyce kept near their big-screen TV. It wasn't until later that he realized what he'd taped over.

The memory of that night shook him. It had been the most incredible sexual experience of his life.

Cynthia released a fire in him that he didn't even

realize he had. The camera, sitting as a silent witness, seemed to magically free him from any inhibition or shame about what they were doing.

Later, alone, he watched the tape.

He could still feel her hands and mouth caressing him, as he watched himself on the screen.

The man on the tape had both fascinated and frightened him.

That man was someone he didn't know.

That man was giving himself in total trust and surrender to a woman, holding nothing back.

That man was *making love*.

He had been both aroused and shaken by what he was seeing. Harlan knew from that night forward, everything was changed. His life with Joyce couldn't be the same, and the future with Cynthia could destroy him.

He'd closed his eyes, trying to blot out the logic that was threatening the heat running through him.

As if she knew, Cynthia had climbed astride him, kissing him, using her body to make him give up any thought of anything except her and their love.

Judge Robinson closed his eyes. Tears ran down his face. He reached for the remote, shutting off the tape and the television. The room filled with a merciful darkness. He sat in it for a long time. Finally he turned on the lamp atop his desk. His eyes went to a framed photograph on the shelf above the television set. He went to it, and picked it up.

Joyce stood smiling in his arms. They were both

dressed in white; shorts and shirts. She held a large, multicolored straw hat.

"Barbados," he said, looking at the picture. She looked happy, her smile as always, warmed him.

Harlan put the photo back on the shelf, and wiped his eyes.

"She's probably at her sister's house," he said out loud. "That's where she is." He went to the desk and reached for the phone. "We've been together too long to end it now. We can work through this," he said. "She'll take me back."

CHAPTER NINETEEN

When Dan Rayner stepped off his private jet from Chicago, he was in handcuffs and accompanied by two uniformed, armed, deputized officers from the Windy City, especially assigned to escort him to Brookport, Massachusetts.

Time had not allowed for officers to travel from Brookport to Chicago and back, and so Officers Lenny Putowski and Richard Saccone, volunteered to make the trip.

The two officers had obviously enjoyed their first, and likely last ride in a private jet. It was clear that on return, tales of this assignment would provide them with many laughs and many drinks back at Billy's, their favorite cop bar.

Mr. Rayner did not share their enthusiasm.

As he and the two officers approached the De-Liberti terminal, he saw Star, Paresi, and Richardson waiting at the gate.

He wasn't happy to see them, either.

Mitchell Grant had found out where Rayner was

from one of his secretaries. Clearly, Rayner hadn't thought to notify his staff that he and Doctor Grant were no longer the closest of friends.

This fact had been brought home just hours before, when Dan opened the door of his suite overlooking the Chicago River and elegant North Michigan Avenue, to find officers Saccone and Putowski brandishing a warrant for his arrest.

Now he sat in interrogation with his three least favorite faces opposite him and his high-priced attorney, Maxwell Clifford, seated at his side.

"Mr. Rayner, do you know why you were arrested in Chicago and returned here?" Star said.

Dan opened his mouth. Max Clifford laid his slim, manicured fingers on his client's arm. "Not a word."

He looked at Star.

"My client and I know a bogus charge when we see it, Lieutenant. Your department is totally in error, and you *will* pay for this."

"Okay," Star said, facing the attorney. "I'll play. Mr. Clifford, your client contracted with the late Willis Henderson to have his wife murdered, and we can prove it."

"Really?" the lawyer said.

"Oh yes." Star turned to Richardson. "Chuck."

The detective got up, left the room, and was back in moments, carrying two folders and two clear plastic bags. One was filled with cash, and the other held the Trailblazer shoe box.

Dan Rayner's face flushed, but he said nothing.

"We do our homework, Counselor," Star said, putting the items on the table.

She pointed to the shoe box.

"That, Mr. Clifford, is a box, which originally held a pair of size twelve Trailblazer shoes."

Max Clifford looked amused.

"And that," Star continued, pointing to the bag of cash, "is two hundred and fifty thousand dollars."

Max Clifford glanced at the money. "And your point is . . ."

"My point is that the Trailblazer shoe box was used to transport and store this money, which was drawn from your client's personal bank account three days before the death of his wife."

"I don't doubt what you're saying, Lieutenant, but I fail to see the connection. Some people like to have cash around the house, and they store money in many containers, including shoe boxes."

"Two hundred and fifty thousand dollars is a lot of petty cash, Mr. Clifford," Star said.

"Mr. Rayner is a *very* wealthy man, Lieutenant," the lawyer said in a tone designed to emphasize that no one on her side of the table could grasp the concept of *real* money. "He often makes large withdrawals."

"Uh-huh," Star said. "And do those large withdrawals always contain the fingerprints of Mr. Rayner, and those of Willis Henderson?"

A cold light flickered in Max Clifford's eyes.

Star continued. "Our experts also matched both sets of prints from the cash to those found on the shoe box."

"Max . . ." Dan Rayner said, his voice edgy.

"Quiet, Dan, it means nothing."

Star turned to Chuck. "Detective Richardson."

"Thank you."

Chuck addressed the attorney. "Mr. Clifford, is it?" he said.

The lawyer stayed silent.

"On the same day that your client withdrew the funds, he also booked a flight on his private jet from DeLiberti to Philadelphia. He checked into a suite of rooms at the Barrington Hotel."

Star opened one of the two folders on the table and laid a copy of the hotel registration in front of them.

"I know what you're going to say. So what?" She smiled at the attorney. "It's not a big deal."

She looked at Dan Rayner; he looked down at the table.

"Except that on this particular date, there happened to be a conference at that hotel; SWAT team members from all around the New England area. They were being briefed on new equipment and new techniques."

She leaned toward the two men. "Now, being a lowly, underfunded police department, of course, we weren't able to finance that trip for *all* of our

SWAT members, so we sent one of our best . . . Willis Henderson."

Rayner looked at his attorney.

Max Clifford regarded Star with cold eyes. "So? You had a rep at a cop's seminar, that means nothing to us."

Star looked at Paresi. "Sergeant Paresi, didn't you have something you wished to present regarding this incident?"

"Yes." Paresi stood. "I do. Be right back." He left the room.

"What kind of stupid game are you playing?" Rayner hissed at Star.

The attorney again put his hand on Dan Rayner's arm. "Quiet, Dan, let me do the talking."

Rayner sat back, glowering at Star with barely contained rage.

Paresi returned with a chestnut-colored, long-limbed, doe-eyed young man, carrying a large, bulky white envelope.

"This is Lerone Moore; he's a bellman at the Barrington, and he remembers meeting Mr. Rayner." He indicated a chair at the table. "Have a seat, Lerone."

"Thank you." The young man sat down next to Chuck, facing Rayner and his attorney. He laid the envelope he was carrying on the table.

Dan Rayner looked at Paresi. "I see a lot of bellmen," he said contemptuously.

"You wanna jog Mr. Rayner's memory, Lerone?" Paresi said.

"Okay." Lerone Moore folded his large hands on top of the envelope. "I got an order for two roast beef dinners, a bottle of Wild Turkey and extra ice, that had to go to Mr. Rayner's suite.

"When I got there, he was with another gentleman, a black gentleman, and they had already had a lot to drink."

"Can you identify the gentleman?" Star said, holding up a photo of Willis Henderson. "Is this the man?"

"Oh yeah, that's him," Lerone said. "I remember, because I'd seen him down in the Stuyvesant Room earlier, with the other police officers."

He beamed at the detectives. "See, I want to be a cop, and when I saw the brother . . . uh, the gentleman, I figured I could talk to him, so I went over, introduced myself, and told him I wanted to do what he did.

"He was real nice. He told me how long he'd been on the force, and how he got on the SWAT team and what they did and all that. He was real friendly, real nice, but that was before he was drinking."

Dan looked at his lawyer. The attorney shook his head, almost imperceptibly, but Star saw it.

"Go on, Lerone."

"Anyway, I could see Mr. Rayner and the other gentleman had been drinking a bit. In fact, Mr. Rayner made me hand him the bottle of Wild Turkey right there at the door, before I even got to the table inside. When I went into the other room to set up the dinner, is when I realized I forgot the extra ice."

"Where were Mr. Rayner and Officer Henderson?" Star said.

"They was in the main room. I was setting up in the dining area, off the living room. When I went back to the kitchen to get the ice, they must have heard me leave and thought I was gone for good.

"Then what happened?"

"Well, I come back in the same way, and I guess they never knew I was there. They got talking real loud, arguing almost, over money."

"How much money?" Star said.

Lerone looked at Dan Rayner. "A lot. I heard Mr. Rayner say, 'I'm paying you two hundred fifty thousand dollars, and I don't want no fuck-ups.' " He looked at Star. "Pardon my language, ma'am, but that's what he said."

"Was either Mr. Rayner or Officer Henderson aware that you might still be in the suite?"

Lerone shook his head. "No, ma'am. They couldn't see me, and to be honest, they had been drinking so much I don't think they could hear me either. They both seemed pretty ticked off about Mr. Rayner's wife."

"How do you know they were talking about Mrs. Rayner?"

"Well, Mr. Rayner, he said, 'I knew when I married her, she was a slut. But I thought I loved her. I couldn't give her up.' "

Rayner's face turned so red, Star thought he might have a stroke.

"Then the other man, the policeman, he said, 'She gon' wreck my friend's life. He can't sleep, he can't eat, his wife is just about crazy anyhow, and this will kill her if she finds out. He'll be finished. Nobody will respect him, and he worked too god-damned hard and sacrificed too fucking much to lose it all for a 'ho. I *will* take the bitch out! She got to go.' " He looked at Star again. "Sorry ma'am, about the cussin'."

"It's okay," Star said. "So, you stayed and listened to everything they said?"

Lerone nodded. "To tell the truth, when I figured out they was talking about killing somebody, I was too scared to move. I figured I best stay put and get out when I felt it was safe."

"You can't be buying this," Maxwell Clifford said. "This man is obviously lying. Why wouldn't he call the police, or tell somebody if he overheard a murder for hire being plotted?"

Lerone faced the lawyer. "I'm not proud that I didn't speak up, sir. But to tell the truth, I was scared."

He pointed to Dan Rayner. "Mr. Rayner is a powerful man. If he could hire somebody to hit his own wife, I don't even want to think about what he could do to me. I tried to tell myself he was drunk, and maybe just talkin', but when she come up dead, I knew then I had to tell what I know."

"Are you still scared of him?" the attorney said.

"Yes sir, I am."

"But you're here, facing him." Max's face reddened. "You don't look scared."

Lerone sat straight in the chair. "I am. I am facing him, and I am scared. But I'm not in this room by myself. I'm facing him with you and the police as witnesses. I don't think anything is going to happen to me now."

He looked back at Star. "Just before I slipped out, I heard Mr. Rayner say, 'Here's a key to my house. She's always home by ten or eleven. You can just wait for her.' "

"Are you sure he said that?" Star said.

"Oh, yes ma'am, I heard him, and that's not all he said."

"Go on," Star said.

"He said, real mean like, 'Don't you fuck up. Remember, I'm paying you a quarter million dollars. I want her *dead*!' "

Rayner turned to his attorney. "*Do something!*"

Max waved his hand dismissively. "Whatever this person has to say doesn't matter, Lieutenant. You know it's hearsay and not admissible in a court of law."

"He's an eyewitness to a conspiracy to commit murder," Star said. "In fact, Counselor, if you want to be technical, Mr. Moore is both an eyewitness and an *earwitness*.

"He *saw* your client and Willis Henderson together, and he *heard* the conversation in which your client solicited and discussed paying Henderson to kill his wife. No judge is going to throw that out."

"It's still hearsay," Max said smugly. "And even if you get a judge to allow it, it comes down to his word against my client's, and who do you think the court will believe?"

"Do you have anything else to say, Lerone?" Star asked.

"No ma'am, only that I saw Mr. Rayner and the policeman again later, just before I went off duty."

"Where?"

Lerone looked at Dan. "I saw them in the lobby. They was still pretty tight, and they was coming out of the bar."

"Did you hear what they were saying?"

"Not all of it . . . just enough to know that the officer was really mad at Mr. Rayner's wife. He said something about white women always fucking things up for the black man."

"And you assumed he was speaking about Mrs. Rayner?"

"No ma'am, I *know* he was, because Mr. Rayner, he said that he knew his wife liked colored men, because she had been with a colored guy when she was in college, before he met her. That's all I heard, they got on the elevator, but I could see their faces . . . both of them looked drunk and mad."

"More hearsay," Max Clifford said.

Star got up. "You know something, Mr. Clifford?

You're right." She turned to Lerone. "Could I have that envelope you brought in from my desk?"

"Yes ma'am." The young man handed her the large white envelope.

Star opened it and took out three videotapes.

Dan Rayner's face went white.

Star waved the tapes in front of Dan Rayner and his attorney.

"I almost forgot. There is another thing money doesn't cushion you from, Mr. Rayner. Big Brother is always watching. In fact, luxury hotels pride themselves on the safety and protection of their guests. You wouldn't believe the technology."

She smiled at Rayner's stricken look. "You never see them, but they are always there, protecting you. In lobbies, hallways . . . *elevators*."

She waved the tapes again. "Your entire conversation in the hall outside the bar," she put one tape down, "the lobby," she put the second tape on top of that one, "and the elevator," she put the third tape on top of the stack, "with Willis Henderson on these three little security tapes."

"You got nothing," Max Clifford said. "They're silent, there's no sound evidence, all you have is two men, in the same area at the same time, exchanging pleasantries and conversation."

"Boy," Star turned to Dan. "Mr. Rayner, you've got yourself some fabulous lawyer. He knows his stuff."

Max Clifford regarded her with cold eyes.

"You're right, Mr. Clifford," Star said, "the tapes are silent, but we've got Dr. Eleanor Maybanks."

"Eleanor Maybanks?" Max Clifford's skin took on a pasty look.

Star nodded. "Yes." She turned toward Dan Rayner. "Dr. Maybanks is the head of the prestigious Coventry College for the Deaf. She is also a board-certified expert lip-reader."

Chuck, Paresi, and Lerone exchanged glances. They were enjoying Star's performance.

"I spoke with her earlier," Star continued, "and she's volunteered her services. In fact, I've had copies of these tapes dubbed for her to view.

"Her board certified status qualifies her as an expert witness, so in a courtroom . . ." She smiled. "Well, you know."

The smirk had long since left Max Clifford's face.

Star turned to the grinning bellman, and shook his hand.

"Thank you, Lerone, for your cooperation. We'll get someone to take you back to the hotel."

He stood, towering over Star's six foot frame, his admiration for her in his eyes. *Stone cold sistuh, go get 'em,* his mind said.

"Thank you," he said. "I'm really enjoying my stay, and I'm glad I could help. You folks have been very kind to me."

"The Philly PD is going to be lucky to get you," Star said.

"I hope so." He grinned. "I'm taking the next test up."

"Good luck." She shook his hand again. "And let me know if you need a recommendation."

"Thank you." Lerone beamed.

"Not at all." Star opened the door. "Just go down this corridor and make a right. There'll be someone in the squad to take you back."

"Thank you, ma'am." He waved to Paresi and Richardson.

"Bye."

The officers waved.

Star closed the door and went back to the table.

"What a nice guy," she said, looking at the stricken faces of Rayner and his attorney. "He's going to make an excellent cop."

She stood over them, smiling. "You guys have to admit, it's been some night for surprises, and guess what?" She reached into her pants pocket. "I've got a few more."

Star held up a small plastic packet.

"Here's a key to Mr. Rayner's home. Both his and Willis Henderson's fingerprints are on it."

"And . . ." She opened the second file on the table. "Here's the CTR from Mr. Rayner's bank."

She handed it to the attorney.

"As you can see, it's official."

Max looked at Dan Rayner. Star caught it.

"Don't be mad at him, Max," she said. "Even though he's richer than God, he still has to follow protocol. The bank will not release anything over ten thousand dollars without a proper Currency Transaction Report. And, as you can see, your client's signature is on the bottom."

Dan Rayner opened his mouth.

"Don't even try it," Star said. "That is *your* signature, not a forgery. You can't send in a ringer to sign this form. . . ." She leaned close to him and smiled. "No matter how rich you are."

Dan Rayner started to cry.

CHAPTER TWENTY

The squad room was practically deserted. The graveyard shift was due to start in less than an hour.

At her desk, Star signed the last report on the evening's events, and handed it to Paresi. He walked it across the room and dropped it into the "In" basket on the table, near Captain Lewis's office door.

"Sometimes I love this job," Star said, leaning back in her chair, stretching.

Richardson closed his desk and crossed the squad room, carrying his overcoat.

"We got that rich, arrogant, racist bastard, and it feels good," he said.

"Amen to that," Paresi said, walking back to his desk. "Ol' Dan couldn't believe it, even when they took him downstairs. Did you see his face?"

Star laughed. "I thought he was going to geyser out right there on the spot."

She stood and took her coat from the rack behind her.

"Did you notice how quickly his lawyer was out

of here? Something tells me Max is calling in a lot of favors tonight. Rayner's probably thinking he'll be sleeping in his own bed before the sun comes up, and let's face it, he just might."

"That's the truth," Chuck said. "Money talks. . . ."

"Yeah, but sometimes nobody listens," Paresi said.

"Let's hope." Chuck nodded.

"Hey," Star said, "even if he's out in time for breakfast, we *still* locked his ass up!"

The three of them slapped palms all around.

"It was good, Star," Chuck said. "Good night."

"Night, Chuck."

With a parting wink, Richardson put on his coat and left the squad room.

Star turned to Paresi.

They looked at one another for a few minutes, smiling.

"Good?" Star said.

"Oh, yeah." Paresi nodded.

They put their coats on in silence.

Paresi picked up his car keys. "Got plans?" he asked.

"Yep."

"Me, too, but breakfast tomorrow?"

"Uh-huh," she said. "Jessie Mae's at seven?"

"It's a date."

She put on her coat. "Oh, don't forget these."

She took the three videotapes from her desk and put them back into the large white envelope. "Vee would strangle me if I lost them."

Paresi held up the envelope. "Just what are these, anyway?"

Star grinned. "One is Lena's sixth birthday party, one is Cole's debut doing his rap routine in the school talent show, and the other one, I think is some cooking show that Vee taped off PBS."

Paresi shook his head. "You're amazing."

"What? I'd never seen Cole's tape, and I love looking at Lena's sixth birthday, she sang for us at that party. You should check it out, there's nothing like a six year old singing "God Bless the Child.""

"You're kidding, right?" Paresi said.

"Oh, no," Star said. "That was Vee's favorite song when she was pregnant with Lena. She sang it all the time; once she was born, Vee sang it to her as a lullaby; so when Lena said she wanted to sing at the party, that's the song that came out. I'm just glad we got it on tape. It's something. Check it out."

Paresi shook his head, grinning.

Star picked up her purse. "And the cooking show was a mistake. I thought I was getting *The Sopranos*."

Paresi tucked the tapes under his arm. "I'll introduce you to my mother's side of the family," he said. "No difference."

They laughed.

"Anyway, make sure Vee gets those. I've had them for weeks." Star settled her purse strap across her shoulder. "While we were waiting for Rayner's plane, I just happened to remember they were in my desk." She smiled. "Came in handy, don't you think?"

CHAPTER TWENTY-ONE

"I can't believe you could turn out something like this in my house where there is no food!" Star said, swirling a fork into a large bowl of linguine with garlic, cheese, spinach, and red peppers. "I get home, you're here, my cat is fed and purring in your lap, and then you do this." She put the food into her mouth. "Mmmmmm, this is so good . . . you really are a magic man."

Mitch dipped into the bowl, twirling pasta onto his fork.

"It's about time you figured that out." He smiled. "As far as being here, I have a key, and Jake and I bonded a long time ago. Besides, I knew you'd be pretty tired, so I wanted you to just be able to take it easy."

He indicated the bowl of pasta. "And as far as this is concerned, I'd like to say what a chore it was, just to impress you with my culinary skills, but I'd be lying. It's pretty basic, and you had enough to throw it together. Even that dreadful grated dried cheese works."

"Paresi made me buy it," Star said, chewing.

"Shame on him. He should give up his Sons of Italy badge; supermarket cheese in a cardboard can." Mitch ate some of the pasta. "Although it is real Romano and Parmesan."

"He made me buy it because he knew fresh cheese would grow hair in my refrigerator," Star said.

"In that case, he's forgiven." Mitch dipped his fork again. "It's not bad. As for the other stuff, it's just some frozen spinach I found in the back of your freezer, with an expiration date that was still in the new century, and a fairly fresh-looking red pepper from the vegetable bin. I found the Mrs. Dash in the cupboard alongside the biggest bottle of hot sauce I've ever seen!"

They laughed.

"It's restaurant size." She grinned. "Jessie Mae got it for me from her supplier in New Orleans . . . it's fierce!"

Mitch nodded. "I'm sure."

Star ate more pasta. "I love this; it's so garlicky."

"That's the Mrs. Dash," Mitch said. "After this, I can no longer be a snob about the stuff. It's a pretty good mix of herbs and garlic. It's a good thing to have around for the cooking-challenged."

"You mean like me," she said, eating more pasta.

"Not *like* you." He grinned. "You."

"I know you would rather we were at your place," she said, again dipping her fork into the bowl.

"For the kitchen, yes," he said. "But for the company, any place with you is just fine with me."

They smiled at one another.

"Besides"—he rolled more pasta onto his fork—"this dish is doable almost anywhere. Its real secret is to put it in the refrigerator and let it chill while you make love for hours."

He swirled more pasta onto his fork. "And with Robin glowering and lurking at my place, I don't think it would have worked." He held his fork out to her.

She ate from it. "Mmmmm-hmmm."

"And . . ." Mitch said, again dipping the fork, "not only is this a very tasty little meal, it provides you with lots of energy and stamina for the long haul. . . ."

He fed her more. "But the best part is that you get to eat it in bed, naked, with the most beautiful woman in the world."

Star's cat, Jake, jumped onto the bed, his pink nose twitching.

"And her cat." Mitch laughed.

Star pulled a strand of olive oil-and-cheese-coated pasta from the bowl and fed it to him.

"He loves pasta," she said.

"He loves the cheese," Mitch said, fishing out another strand.

Star grinned. "What he really loves is garlic."

"No." Mitch shook his head. "Cats don't eat garlic!"

"This one does," Star said, feeding Jake another long, thin noodle.

"Then you're going to enjoy living at my house, Jake," Mitch said to the cat. I have braids of the stuff hanging in my kitchen."

Star leaned her bare shoulder against his chest, enjoying the softness of the thick hair there. "We talked about that," she said. "I like having my own place."

"I know." Mitch swirled more pasta onto his fork. "But you also spend a lot of time with me, so why not just pack up the cat and move? Think how happy Jake would be. He'd get to see you all the time. I know he misses you when you sleep over. He told me tonight, while we were waiting for you."

"He told you?" Star said, grinning.

"Yes." Mitch nodded. "Didn't you know I'm quite fluent in Catspeak?"

Star laughed. "Another hidden talent?"

"You've only just begun to explore the surface of my gifts, darlin'," Mitch said.

The look in his eyes made her blush all over.

"Well, *darlin'*," Star said, "as fascinating as that is, and as anxious and curious as I am to begin my exploration, I think we're going to have to postpone things, at least for a little while. There's somebody else in the mix right now. You've got to get things straight with your daughter. Until that's settled, moving in together is not an option."

Mitch looked at her for a minute. "Kiss me," he said.

Star smiled. "Garlic breath and all?"

He nodded. "Garlic breath and all."

They kissed.

Jake's cold nose on the back of her hand broke them up. The cat, prowling stealthily atop the covers, had finally landed in Star's lap, heading toward the bowl of pasta.

"No more for you." She handed the bowl to Mitch and picked up the cat. "You're going out."

He watched her as she padded barefoot and naked across the floor, carrying the cat like an infant. At the door, she stroked Jake's back and head, deposited him outside the room, and closed the door.

Mitch watched her walk back to the bed.

"He never scratches you, does he?"

"Nope." She got under the covers, her body warm against his. "Jake has no idea he's a cat," she said, snuggling.

An indignant howl echoed from outside the door.

"Well he knows he's sad. He wants to be in here."

"He'll get over it." She reached for the bowl.

"Later." Mitch set it on the nightstand next to the bed.

"I'm still hungry," she said.

"Me, too." He reached for her.

Robin Grant sat in the middle of her father's huge bed with her legs folded beneath her, yoga style, talking to her friend Tiffany in Rhode Island.

"He left hours ago, and I know he's not coming back tonight." Robin cradled the phone between her shoulder and neck, and reached for the bottle on the night table.

"I know . . . I will," she said. "No, I don't know *how* I'm going to do it, Tif, but you can bet your ass I'm *going* to do it," she said forcefully. "I'm going to break this cozy little setup into a million pieces."

She took a drink from the bottle. A particularly fine vintage of Pouilly-Fuissé, which she had liberated from her father's wine keep.

"Yeah, my mom is humiliated, and you know what a bitch she is, even under the best of circumstances. She's been calling here every five minutes all night, and she's more and more pissed with each call."

She sipped more wine. "No, I didn't tell her where he is . . . I can't! She knows anyway, she just wants to bust his balls, and since he's not here, the bitch juice rains down on me."

She drank again. "Yeah, I thought about it, but if I tell her, she'll say something to him, then he'll go ballistic and cut her off . . . correction, cut *us* off. I can't let that happen."

Robin listened to her friend.

"Yes he will." She listened some more.

"I know, Tif. . . . I know how cool he looks, but believe me, my mom can push all of his buttons. She can make him lose it, and trust me, that's *not* a pretty sight." She drank some more. "No, I can't see him getting over this one. She's different. The truth is this thing looks plenty serious."

"Marry her? No, that's not going to happen."

She drained the bottle and burped.

"I won't let that happen."

Chuck Richardson looked in on his sleeping son.

Chuck Junior lay on his stomach, his long pajama-clad body diagonally across his bed, with one arm hanging down. His relaxed, hoop-shooting fingers nearly touched the floor.

Chuck went in and gently righted his son in the bed.

Chuck Junior said something in sleep gibberish and curled up on his side, his knees tucked up near his chest.

His father kissed his slightly damp cheek, covered him up again, and left the room.

It had been quite a night. Chuck took off his shoulder holster and hung it on a peg in the closet. He put his Glock into the nightstand next to his side of the bed, and locked it.

With his son in the house, he wanted to have a weapon for protection, but he had to be safe, too.

Even though Chuck Junior was nearly sixteen, and knew all about guns, Chuck still locked his weapon away when he came home.

He kept the key on his ring; it was always with him. He slept with his keys under his wife's pillow. If an intruder got in, he could get them, open that drawer, and be armed in seconds.

He looked at his bed. Arlene wouldn't have liked the idea of the gun in the drawer. She'd never gotten used to his being a cop, anyway. But she was gone, ten years now, lost to cancer, leaving him with a son to raise, alone.

He sat down on the bed. The image of Cynthia Chapin-Rayner standing dead in that pit invaded his mind.

Chuck clasped his hands together between his knees. He closed his eyes tightly, trying to squeeze the picture from his psyche. In its place, Dan Rayner's smug face across the interrogation room table appeared.

"Son of a bitch!" Chuck whispered. *How could he do that?* How could a man want his wife dead? If the marriage was shit, then why not just get a divorce? Why kill her like that?

A coldness washed over him.

"And Willis . . ." Chuck said out loud. "How could he? He was a cop, he took an oath to protect and serve and uphold the law, how could he kill a woman so viciously, and for money?"

* * *

The short drive to Joyce's sister's house was the most difficult one he'd ever had to make. When he called, his wife of twenty years refused to speak to him, and now Harlan Dubois Robinson stood on the doorstep, afraid to ring the bell.

From inside, he could hear the sound of Billie Holiday. Joyce always listened to Billie when she needed to think, to "de-stress," as she put it. Harlan convinced himself it was a good sign.

He rang the front doorbell.

The music stopped.

Through the thin gauze curtain covering the square of cut glass in the door, he could see the faint outline of a woman approaching.

She opened the door.

It was Joyce's sister, Saranell.

"She don't want to see you," the woman said, her voice low and even.

"Can I come in?" Harlan said.

"No." Saranell's face was still, her anger frozen behind her eyes.

"Saranell, please . . . just tell her all I need is a minute, just one minute," Harlan pleaded.

"Go away," the woman said. "My sister don't need no sorry-ass dog like you messing up her life."

Saranell started to shut the door. Harlan grabbed it, pushing it back, holding it open.

"Please, Saranell, tell her I only want a minute," he pleaded.

"It's okay, Saranell." Joyce appeared behind her sister. "I'll hear him out."

"You don't need to listen to this piece of shit," Saranell said from between clenched teeth. "He done hurt you enough."

"It's okay." Joyce moved in front of her sister. Saranell remained rooted to the spot, her dark eyes locked on Harlan.

"Can we talk, baby?" he said to his wife. "Can we go somewhere, just the two of us, and talk this out?"

Joyce just stared at him, and with a speed that surprised all of them, she struck.

The sound of the slap cracked into the quiet like sudden thunder on a summer's day.

Harlan reeled back, his eyes watering, his ears ringing. He tasted blood in his mouth.

"Joyce!"

Behind her, Saranell smiled.

"Baby . . . please . . ." he said, numbly, his voice straining through his loosened teeth like rusty water through a clogged grate.

Joyce Robinson stood like stone.

"Please . . ." Harlan said again.

Without any emotion, she stepped close, spit in his face, and slammed the door.

Dan Rayner sat on a lumpy, dirty mattress on a cot in the men's lockup in the bowels of the Seventeenth Precinct. His attorney, Max Clifford, was arranging his bail, and not a moment too soon. He didn't care what price they set, he could meet it. All he wanted was out.

The smell of Lysol was not living up to its advertising. There was nothing fresh or clean smelling about this toilet. He had to get out, and soon. He was cold, and he needed a drink.

He ran his hand over the rough, woolen blanket folded at the foot of the cot. "No way." He crossed his arms across his chest.

"I can't fucking believe this," he muttered to himself.

"My good friend Grant tells the pigs where I am, and then his fucking whore does *this* to me!"

His legs jiggled uncontrollably. "I'm gonna show them . . . they won't get away with this. . . ."

Sweat ran from his forehead into his eyes. He wiped his trembling fingers across them. "Fucking Mitch . . . I'll bury him, and that whore. Goddamn niggers . . . not worth the breath in their bodies."

He wiped his mouth. "That's what I get for picking one to do the job . . . all he did was fuck up!"

His mind went back to his first meeting with Willis Henderson at the hotel. Dan had seen Willis with a group of other SWAT members in the hotel lobby when he arrived.

There was something about the tall, strong-looking black man that caught his eye. . . . Willis was a man he figured his wife would have gone for, and so, hours later, after they'd both had a few, the billionaire approached the cop in the hotel bar.

It was there that Dan learned of Willis's ties with Brookport and that asshole judge his wife was fucking. Things couldn't have been more perfect. Dan felt that Fate had put him in just the right spot to bring an end to his dilemma.

"I should never have trusted that black bastard," he said between gritted teeth. "He fucked everything up."

Dan's tongue felt thick and furry. He wiped more sweat from his face.

"That stupid prick left every fucking thing but a signed picture with his address on the back."

Dan rubbed his cheek, listening to the sandpapery sound of his beard growing.

How long had he been in this rat hole? He *really* needed a drink. He blinked. Willis Henderson was standing in front of him.

"Fucking trained mercenary my ass," he shouted at the apparition. "Your own wife took you out!"

He blinked again. Willis disappeared.

Dan looked down at his laceless shoes. They'd taken his belt and shoelaces when he was booked. Some asshole thought he would be a suicide risk. Like hell, he thought. He wasn't offing himself over this shit. There was no way he was leaving the planet, and there was no way he was doing any time. He was too old, too tired, and much too fucking rich.

* * *

Dominic Paresi lay with his head on Vee's breast, enjoying the heat and softness of her plump body and the feel of her fingers in his hair.

"I'm glad you're not still mad at me," he said.

Vee laughed. "Who said I'm not?"

Paresi kissed her breast, and ran the tip of his tongue over her erect nipple. "She does," he said, sucking the firm, raisin-colored bud gently between his lips.

Vee sighed, her back arched beneath him.

Paresi moved on top of her. "What am I going to do with you gone?"

"It's not forever," Vee said, her voice as soft and warm as her skin. "It's just a week. Star and I planned this a long time ago. We need to do it."

Paresi kissed her neck, her shoulders. "Suppose I asked you not to go."

"You can ask. . . ." Vee said, smiling. "In fact, why don't you try to convince me to stay?"

"Is that a challenge?" Paresi's blue eyes twinkled.

Vee nodded.

"Well . . . I'm always up for that."

Mitch lay in Star's arms, his head on her shoulder.

"Are you alright?" she asked.

"Just thinking."

"About?"

"Dan . . . tonight, the way you arrested him."

He was quiet for a moment and when he spoke, his voice seemed to come from far away.

"I can't believe he had Cyn killed."

Star didn't say anything, she just held him tighter. Finally she spoke. "Believe it or not, I'm really sorry about your friend."

"He's not my friend," Mitch said. "The guy that did that is not anybody I ever knew. My friend must have died a long time ago."

He was quiet again. She stroked his face and ran her fingers through his hair.

"I wish you'd reconsider what you're planning," he said finally.

"It'll just be for a little while." Star's voice was soft. "You need to spend time with your daughter, and I need a break."

He kissed her neck. "*We* should be taking this trip, not you and Vee."

She hugged him. "Your daughter needs you right now."

"That's really hard to believe," Mitch said.

"She's angry, and she's acting out because she wants your attention. You need to get past her behavior and talk to her. She's in pain, and you both need to face it. She's a very angry and disturbed girl."

"That's her mother's fault," Mitch said.

"Maybe." Star put her fingers in his hair. "But

you're her father, and she needs to know that you love her."

She kissed him gently.

"I'll only be away for a week. You'll live."

"Don't be so sure."

CHAPTER TWENTY-TWO

"Good morning, Red Rose Travel Agency," the male voice said.

"Good morning, my name is Verenita Spencer-Martin, and I made reservations for a trip for my friend and me to Hawaii."

"Yes? Is there a problem?"

"A little one," Vee said. "When we made the reservations, we asked to be seated together, and the tickets that arrived this morning have us on opposite ends of the plane. When the agent gave me the information, he said we were together, so somebody goofed somewhere."

"Let me look into that," the voice said. "May I have your name again?"

"Verenita Spencer-Martin," Vee said. "I've got a number, will that help?"

"Very much," the man said.

"Okay . . ." Vee looked at the number on the confirmation letter. "It's ASV67832."

"ASV67832," the man repeated.

Vee could hear the clicking of computer keys.

"Here it is," he said. "I've got it . . . Verenita Spencer-Martin, and Starletta Duvall."

"That's us."

"Well, obviously there's been some error," the man said. "I'll take care of it for you. It's on the original order as seats One A and Two A, so that should put you right together."

"Anything you can do would be appreciated," Vee said.

"Oh, I'll make sure you're together, and because you're being so nice about *our* mistake, I'm going to give you an upgrade. The plane is not fully booked, and there are two seats available in first class."

"Wow!" Vee beamed. "Thank you so much. That's wonderful. My friend is a tall woman, and she's not too crazy about coach seats. She always tries for the bulkhead, so that she can stretch her legs. We thought we had it on this flight, until I saw the tickets."

"You should have had it," the man said, but the mix-up is in your favor. First class beats the bulkhead. It's very comfortable, even professional basketball players can stretch out and relax."

Vee laughed. "She's not *that* tall, but she'll really be happy to hear about this. Thank you again."

"No problem," the man said. "You'll be flying on the twenty-third, correct?"

"Yes," Vee said.

"Sounds like fun. You and your friend are going at a perfect time."

"Well, we both have pretty stressful jobs, and we needed some time away. We've been friends since we were children, and this is the first time we've ever gone away alone, just the two of us."

"I know you'll have a great time," he said. "May I ask what you ladies do?"

"I'm an accountant, and she's a police officer."

"A police officer, wow, that sounds exciting."

"Oh it is," Vee said. "She's a lieutenant and she works homicide."

"Homicide?" the man said. "That must be difficult, I would think, but still very exciting."

"Yes, it is," Vee said. "But it's wearing on the nerves. We're so looking forward to this."

"While you're on the line, let me just recheck your hotel accommodations."

"Okay."

"Let's see here. You'll actually be staying on Kilauea," he said. "That's good, that's away from the mainland, and much nicer than being right in the thick of things."

There was more clicking of keys. "The downside is there is a volcano," the man said, laughing.

"We know." Vee laughed with him. "But we're pretty sure we'll be safe. We mainly chose Kilauea because of the wildlife preserve. My friend loves big cats and so we're going to see them."

"You don't sound too happy about the cats," the agent said.

"I'm not, really." Vee laughed. "But they have other things I want to see, so we compromised."

"Sounds like a tight friendship."

"We're like sisters."

"That's wonderful. You'll love the wildlife preserve. It's very impressive."

"Have you been there?" Vee asked.

"No, but I've seen a lot of pictures." He clicked more keys. "Here you are, you're staying at the Mahalo. That's a great place. They have individual cabins, very private and it's on the beach."

"We're really looking forward to that," Vee said.

"Uh-huh . . . let's see here . . . you're in bungalow twelve, two queen-sized beds, and a deck with a hot tub."

"That's us," Vee said.

"As I said, it's on the water, and it has a view of the volcano."

"Good, then if I see smoke, we *will* be packing," Vee said.

They laughed together.

"It'll be great. You ladies have a good time."

"Thank you so much," Vee said. "You've been very nice. May I have your name, so that I can tell your supervisor how courteous and helpful you've been?"

"Oh, thank you," he said. "We aren't allowed to give out our names, but my number is 1074."

"1074," Vee said. "Got it. Can you transfer me to your boss?"

"No ma'am, but I can give you an 800 number."

"Okay."

"It's 800-683-8872."

"800-683-8872," Vee said.

"Yes ma'am."

"I'll make the call right now; thank you again."

Number 1074 clicked the mouse and printed out two copies of the plane and hotel information for Verenita Spencer-Martin and Starletta Duvall.

He had always been lucky. Well, almost always. If you didn't count his current circumstances. Still, it was a break. Today was his last day on the phones. He was leaving in two days, and now he knew exactly where he was going.

He'd thought about the day he'd leave for a long time, but he'd never expected his job to give him so much to look forward to.

When Red Rose Travel first approached the warden about using prison labor to work the travel phones, it had taken some convincing. But in the end, though most of the public didn't know it, the travel lines were worked almost exclusively from the prison, by inmates.

At the end of his shift, number 1074 went back to his cell and carefully unfolded his copy of the travel itinerary he'd printed out for Ms. Spencer-Martin and Ms. Duvall.

He'd only had a glimpse or two of Ms. Spencer-Martin, but he knew Ms. Duvall . . . Lieutenant Duvall very well. He'd thought of her practically every waking moment, since he'd been on the inside.

Now, due to good behavior and the fact that the parole board was heavy with women, he was on his way out, and what better way to begin his new freedom, than with a trip to Hawaii. He laughed. Hell, he wouldn't even be leaving the country!

He looked at the calendar on his wall. He had about a week before their departure to get things set up.

As soon as he was on the other side of the gate, he was going to call the Mahalo on Kilauea. He'd booked other clients there, so he knew practically everybody working the desk.

"I think I'll speak to Larisa," he said. "She likes my voice, and I know she wants to meet me."

He sat on his bunk, his mind racing. "Bungalow twelve. Maybe I should ask for number ten; close, but not too close. I want to keep the element of surprise." He laughed.

"Wait till she sees me again." He lay back on the bunk. "And she's got a friend. Two for the price of one. I'd better rest up and eat my Wheaties."

Restless with the thought of his release and the trip, he got up and looked in the mirror over the steel sink.

He turned, looking first at the right and then

the left side of his body. He worked out daily in the gym; he was buffed, but it wasn't his physique he was worried about.

He stared at his face. There were a few lines; prison tended to do that, but he was still a very handsome man. His black hair, grown long since he was inside, cascaded over his shoulders and nearly down to his shoulder blades.

The guys called him "Cochise." He liked that. He liked his hair long. Back in the day, he kept it that way, and wore it in a ponytail, but the boss at his last place of employment had made him cut it. It didn't change anything, he still got more pussy than any man had a right to.

"Pussy," he said out loud, licking his lips. "It's been a long, dry spell, detective." He pulled his hair back, studying his face.

It reflected a hardness. "Cost me some, but I haven't let anybody in here touch me . . ." he said to his reflection. "I've been saving it all up . . . just for you."

He turned his head. She'd never seen him with long hair. It would be an added bonus. She'd never recognize him . . . at least, not right away, and then . . . well, she'd dig it.

He took a deep breath, a little stitch in his side bent him over the sink.

"Mmmmmm," he said, pressing on the rib. "God-damned thing never did heal right."

His reflection stared back at him with steel gray eyes.

"I can't wait to see you again, *Deteckative* Lieutenant Starletta Duvall. We're going to have some fucking great reunion."

His hand snaked down the front of his prison-issue pants.

"I got *big* plans for you."

He threw back his long hair, and laughed.

Don't miss more cases solved
by Starletta Duvall!

GREEN MONEY

by Judith Smith-Levin

For homicide detective Lieutenant Starletta
Duvall and her partner, Dominic Parisi, the
torching of a homeless woman is a random act
of unspeakable violence. The autopsy, however,
turns up an enigmatic calling card, suggesting
that the crime scene's chilling proximity to the
exclusive prep school is no coincidence. Before
Star and Dom can prove their gut instincts,
another corpse is found. When the killer delivers
the third victim gift-wrapped, a lethal and
increasingly perverse game seems afoot.

But appearances can be deceiving. . . .

Published by Fawcett Books.
Available at bookstores everywhere.